HEIDI

HEIDI

by Johanna Spyri

Illustrated in Black and White

Cover illustration by Anita Nelson

J. G. Ferguson Publishing Company
Chicago, Illinois

Printed in the United States of America
ISBN 0-89434-124-3
P-3

Contents

Illustrations

Introduction

Heidi is the story of an orphaned little girl who is taken to live with her grandfather high up on a mountain in Switzerland. Heidi's life on the mountain is healthful, joyful, and simple: she drinks fresh goat's milk and eats toasted cheese and bread; she spends her days playing on the mountainside with Peter the goatherd and his goats; and she sleeps soundly every night on her bed of fresh hay gazing out her little round window at the stars.

But one day she is taken to Frankfurt to live with a wealthy family as a companion for the invalid daughter, Clara. Heidi's forthright honesty and her ignorance of the refined manners of city life get her into trouble with the stern housekeeper, Miss Rottenmeier, and make for some amusing incidents. Although Heidi and Clara become fast friends, and Heidi is by nature a happy child, she nevertheless becomes homesick for her grandfather and the mountains; eventually she returns home.

Heidi was written in 1880 by Johanna Spyri (1829–1901). Spyri was born in a small village called

Hirzel, near Zurich, in Switzerland, and she and her five brothers and sisters grew up in surroundings much like she describes in *Heidi*. Her father was a country doctor, her mother a poet. Like Heidi, she spent her youth amid fields of wildflowers, tending the goats. This life taught her a deep appreciation of nature and a love of animals and books, as well as gave her an understanding of the sufferings of the sick.

When Spyri married, she and her husband went to live in Zurich, where he was the town clerk. About this time she began to write stories to raise money for wounded refugees of the Franco-Prussian war. *Heidi* was her first long story, and it was an immediate success. It was translated into English from its original German in 1884.

While Heidi is obviously the main character of the book (she appears in nearly every scene), just as central to the appeal and meaning of the story are the mountains, which not only provide the setting, but play a part in the outcome as well.

Switzerland is a land of mountains; more than half of its area is covered by their steep ridges, forested slopes, meadows, and snow-covered crags. The air there is famous for being especially healthful for people with tuberculosis (a disease that most often affects the lungs) because it is generally dry and germfree, and consequently many health resorts are located there. In addition, many people travel far to hike, ski, and climb Switzerland's mountains. There are two major mountain chains in Switzerland, the Jura in the northwest part of the country, and the Alps in the southeast. The Alps are by far the grandest of the two, with many steep gorges, waterfalls, and some of the highest peaks in the world, including the famous Matterhorn, 14,691 feet high. Zurich, where Spyri did her writing, is located between the two mountain ranges in a plateau region called the Mittelland. The majority of the Swiss people live in the Mittelland where there are many lakes as well as the richest farmland.

In *Heidi*, Spyri created a character as fresh and inspiring as her beloved mountains. Indeed, Heidi seems to bring a breath of healthful mountain air into the lives of everyone she meets: stern, aloof Alm Uncle softens and welcomes people back into his life; blind Grandmother is cheered by Heidi's chatter; wheelchair-bound Clara regains her health; and the morose Doctor finds a reason for living.

The theme of the book revolves around Heidi's simple, inspiring faith: trust in God; good things come to those who say their prayers and believe that God will grant them what is best for them. Heidi's kindness, sincerity, and positive outlook make her an appealing character—one that any child would want for a friend.

One great gift Heidi is given in Frankfurt is having been taught how to read. In her moments of homesickness she turns to the book of Bible stories that Clara's grandmother has given her, "delighted with the new world that was open to her as the black letters grew alive and turned into men and things and exciting stories." It became her chief pleasure "to read the tales which belonged to the beautiful pictures over and over again."

It is with the same delight that we read *Heidi*. Whatever our situation in life, wherever we live, there are times when we long to be somewhere else. Good books can take us anywhere we want to go; the places they describe and the characters they depict become so real to us that we can later recall scenes as if they were our own memories. As you read *Heidi*, can you see the sun "setting fire" to the snow covered mountains as it sets? Can you hear the roar of the wind in the fir trees? Can you taste the warm, creamy toasted cheese Heidi eats for her supper? Can you feel the soft, rustling hay as she goes to sleep? Come now to Switzerland and play with Heidi and the goats in a sunny alpine meadow full of flowers. And when you are finished, just see if you haven't brought a little of Heidi's happy life back with you and made it your own.

Up the Mountain to Alm-Uncle

THE pleasant old village of Mayenfeld lies in a valley at the foot of lofty mountains. From it a footpath leads through shady, green meadow to the mountains and on up to their summit. As the path ascends, the land grows wilder and the meadow grasses soon give place to mountain plants.

On a clear, sunny morning in June a tall, strong-looking girl climbed up the path, leading a little girl by the hand. The child's cheeks were so aglow with heat that the crimson color could be seen even through the dark, sunburned skin. This was hardly to be wondered at, for in spite of the hot June sun she was clothed as if to keep off the bitterest frost. She did not look more than five years old, if as much, but what her natural figure was like it would have been hard to say. She had on apparently two, if not three, dresses, one above the other, and over these a thick, red, woolen shawl wound round about her, so that her little body presented a shapeless appearance. Her

1

small feet were shod in thick, nailed mountain shoes. Slowly and laboriously she plodded along in the heat. The two must have left the valley a good hour's walk behind them when they came to the hamlet known as Dörfli, which is situated halfway up the mountain. Here they were greeted from all sides. Some of the villagers called to them from windows, some from open doors, others from outside, for the elder girl was now in her old home. She did not, however, pause in her walk to respond to her friends' welcoming cries and questions, but passed on without stopping for a moment until she reached the last of the scattered houses of the hamlet.

Here a voice called to her from the door: "Wait a moment, Dete; if you are going up higher, I will come with you."

The girl stood still, and the child immediately let go her hand and sat down on the ground.

"Are you tired, Heidi?" asked her companion.

"No, I am hot," answered the child.

"We shall soon get to the top now. You must walk bravely on a little longer, and take good long steps, and in another hour we shall be there," said Dete in an encouraging voice.

They were now joined by a stout, good-natured-looking woman, who walked on ahead with her old acquaintance. The two at once began a lively conversation about everybody and everything in Dörfli and its surroundings, while the child wandered on behind them.

"And where are you off to with the child?" asked the one who had just joined the party. "I suppose it is the child your sister left?"

"Yes," answered Dete. "I am taking her up to Uncle, where she must stay."

"The child stay up there with Alm-Uncle! You must be out of your senses, Dete! How can you think of such a thing? The old man, however, will soon send you and your proposal packing off home again!"

"He cannot very well do that, seeing that he is her grandfather. He must do something for her. I have had the charge of the child till now, and I can tell you, Barbel, I am not going to let her keep me from taking the place I have had offered to me. It is for the grandfather now to do his duty by her."

"That would be all very well if he were like other people," said stout Barbel warmly, "but you know what he is. And what can he do with a child, especially with one so young! The child cannot possibly live with him. But where are you thinking of going yourself?"

"To Frankfurt, where an extra good place awaits me," answered Dete. "The people I am going to were down at the Baths last summer, and I took care of their rooms. They would have liked then to take

me away with them, but I could not leave. Now they
are there again and have repeated their offer, and I
intend to go with them."

"I am glad I am not the child!" exclaimed Barbel,
with a gesture of horrified pity. "Not a creature
knows anything about the old man up there! He
will have nothing to do with anybody, and never sets
his foot inside a church from one year's end to another. When he does come down once in a while,
everybody clears out of the way of him and his big
stick. The mere sight of him, with his bushy, gray
eyebrows and his immense beard, is alarming enough.
He looks like any old heathen or Indian, and few
would care to meet him alone."

"Well, and what of that?" said Dete, in a defiant
voice. "He is the grandfather all the same, and must
look after the child. He is not likely to do her any
harm, and if he does, he will have to answer for it,
not I."

"I should very much like to know," said Barbel,
"what the old man has on his conscience that he looks
as he does, and lives up there on the mountain like a
hermit, hardly ever allowing himself to be seen. All
kinds of things are said about him. Didn't you learn
a good deal about him from your sister?"

"Yes, I did, but I am not going to repeat what I
heard. If it should come to his ears I should get into
trouble about it."

Now Barbel had for a long time been most anxious to learn particulars about Alm-Uncle. She could not understand why he seemed to feel such hatred toward his fellow creatures, and insisted on living all alone, or why people spoke about him half in whispers, as if afraid to say anything against him, and yet unwilling to take his part. Moreover, Barbel was in ignorance as to why all the people in Dörfli called him "Alm-Uncle," for he could not possibly be uncle to everybody living there. Barbel had lived in Dörfli only since her marriage, which had taken place not long before. Previous to that her home had been below in Prättigau. For this reason she was not well acquainted with all the events that had ever taken place in Dörfli and its neighborhood.

Dete, on the contrary, had been born in Dörfli, and had lived there until her mother's death the year before. She had then gone over to the Baths at Ragatz and taken service in the large hotel as chambermaid. Barbel knew that Dete could tell her all about Alm-Uncle and she was therefore determined not to lose this good opportunity of satisfying her curiosity. She put her arm through Dete's in a confidential sort of way, and said: "I know I can find out the real truth from you, and the meaning of all these tales that are afloat about him. Tell me what is wrong with the old man, and if he was always shunned as now."

"If I was sure that what I told you would not go

the whole round of Prättigau," said Dete, "I could
relate all kinds of things about him. My mother came
from Domleschg, and so did he."

"Why, Dete, what do you mean?" asked Barbel,
somewhat offended. "Gossip has not reached such a
dreadful pitch in Prättigau as all that, and I am quite
capable of holding my tongue when it is necessary."

"Very well then, I will tell you—but just wait a
moment," said Dete in a warning voice. She looked
back to make sure that the child was not near enough
to hear all she was going to relate, but the little girl
was nowhere to be seen. She had wandered away
sometime before, while her companions were too
eagerly occupied with their conversation to notice it.
Dete stood still and looked around her in all directions. The footpath wound a little here and there,
but could nevertheless be seen along its whole length
nearly to Dörfli. No one, however, was visible upon
it at the moment.

"I see where she is," exclaimed Barbel. "Look!"
She pointed to a spot far away from the footpath.
"She is climbing up the slope over there with the goatherd and his goats. I wonder why he is so late today
bringing them up. It happens well, however, for us,
for now he can look after the child, and you can the
better tell me your tale."

"Oh, as to the looking after," remarked Dete, "the
boy need not put himself out about that. Heidi is

not by any means stupid for her five years, and she knows how to use her eyes. She notices all that is going on, and learns quickly, and it is a good thing, for she will have to look out for herself someday. The old man has nothing to leave her but his two goats and his hut."

"Did he ever have more?" asked Barbel.

"I should think so indeed," replied Dete with animation. "He was owner once of one of the largest farms in Domleschg, but he tried to play the grand gentleman and he soon drank and gambled away his property. Having nothing left to him but his bad name, he disappeared. After many years he came back to Domleschg, bringing with him a young child, whom he tried to place with some of his relatives. Every door, however, was shut in his face, for no one wished to have anything more to do with him. Embittered by this treatment, he vowed never to set foot in Domleschg again, and he then came to Dörfli.

"His son, Tobias, became a carpenter. He was a steady lad, and kindly received by everyone in Dörfli. The old man, however, was still looked upon with suspicion, and there were many strange rumors about him. We, however, did not refuse to acknowledge our relationship with him. You see, my great-grandmother on my mother's side had been his grandmother's sister. So we called him 'Uncle,' and soon he became known all over the place as Uncle. Since

he went to live on the Alm he has been known everywhere as 'Alm-Uncle.' "

"And what happened to Tobias?" asked Barbel,
who was listening with deep interest.

"Wait a moment, I am coming to that," replied
Dete. "Tobias was taught his trade in Mels, and
when he had served his apprenticeship, he came back
to Dörfli and married my sister Adelheid, but their
happiness did not last long. Tobias met with his
death only two years after their marriage. A beam
fell upon him as he was working, and killed him on
the spot. They carried him home, and when Adelheid saw the poor, disfigured body of her husband
she was so overcome with horror and grief that she
fell into a fever from which she never recovered.
And so, two months after Tobias died, his wife followed him.

"Their sad fate was the talk of everybody. People
thought it was a punishment which Uncle had deserved for the godless life he had led. All at once we
heard that he had gone to live up the Alm and did not
intend ever to come down again. Since then he has
led his solitary life on the mountainside, at enmity
with God and man.

"Mother and I took Adelheid's little one, Heidi,
then only a year old. When mother died last year,
and I went down to the Baths to earn some money, I
paid old Ursel, who lives in the village just above, to

take care of Heidi. I stayed on at the Baths through the winter. Early in the spring the same family I had waited on before returned from Frankfurt, and again asked me to go back with them, as I told you. And so we leave the day after tomorrow, and I can assure you it is an excellent place for me."

"And you are going to give the child over to the old man up there? It surprises me beyond words that you can think of doing such a thing, Dete," said Barbel, in a voice full of reproach.

"What do you mean?" demanded Dete. "I have done my duty by the child, and what would you have me do with her now? I certainly cannot take a child five years old with me to Frankfurt. But where are you going, Barbel? We are now halfway up the Alm."

"We have just reached the place I wanted," answered Barbel. "I had something to say to the goatherd's wife, who does some spinning for me in the winter. So good-by, Dete, and good luck to you!"

Dete shook hands with her friend and stood looking after her as she went toward a small, dark-brown hut, which stood a few steps away from the path in a hollow that afforded it some protection from the mountain wind.

Here lived Peter the little eleven-year-old goatherd. Every morning he went down to Dörfli to get the goats and drive them up on the mountain, where they were free to browse till evening on the delicious mountain plants. Then Peter, with his light-footed animals, would go running and leaping down the mountain again till he reached Dörfli. There he would give a shrill whistle through his fingers, whereupon all the owners of the goats would come out to take home the animals that belonged to them.

Peter's father, who had also been known as the goatherd, had been accidentally killed while cutting wood some years before. His mother, whose real name was Brigitta, was always called "the goatherd's wife," for the sake of old association, while the blind grandmother was just "grandmother" to all the old and young in the neighborhood.

Dete stood for a good ten minutes looking about her in every direction for some sign of the children and the goats. Not a glimpse of them, however, was to be seen, so she climbed to a higher spot, where she could get a fuller view of the mountain as it sloped beneath her to the valley. With ever-increasing anxiety on her face and in her movements, she continued to scan the surrounding slopes.

Meanwhile the children were climbing up by a roundabout way, for Peter knew many spots where all kinds of good food grew for his goats. Heidi, exhausted with the heat and weight of her thick armor of clothes, panted and struggled after him, at first, with some difficulty. She said nothing, but her bright

eyes kept watching first Peter, as he sprang nimbly
hither and thither on his bare feet clad only in his
short, light breeches, and then the slim-legged goats
that went leaping over rocks and shrubs and up the
steep ascents with even greater ease! All at once she
sat down on the ground, and as fast as her little fingers
could move, began pulling off her shoes and stockings.
This done she rose, unwound the hot, red shawl and
threw it away, and then proceeded to undo her frock.
It was off in a second, but there was still another to
unfasten, for Dete had put the Sunday frock on over
the everyday one, to save the trouble of carrying it.
Quick as lightning the everyday frock followed the
other. The child stood up, clad only in her light,
short-sleeved undergarment, and stretched out her little bare arms with glee. She put all her clothes together in a neat heap, and then went jumping and
climbing up after Peter and the goats as nimbly as
any of them.

Peter had not noticed what the child was doing
when she stayed behind, but when she ran up to him
in her new attire, his face broke into a grin, which
grew broader still as he looked back and saw the small
heap of clothes lying on the ground. He said nothing, however.

The child began at once to ask Peter many questions. She wanted to know how many goats he had,
where he was going with them, and what he had to do

when he arrived there. At last, after some time, they approached the hut and came within view of Dete.

As soon as she caught sight of the little company climbing up toward her she shrieked out: "Heidi, what have you been doing? What a sight you have made yourself! And where are your two frocks and the red scarf? And the new shoes I bought, and the new stockings I knitted for you—everything gone! Not a thing left! What can you have been thinking of, Heidi? Where are all your clothes?"

The child quietly pointed to a spot below on the mountainside and answered, "Down there."

Dete followed the direction of her finger. She could just distinguish something lying on the ground, with a spot of red on the top of it which she had no doubt was the woolen scarf.

"You good-for-nothing little thing!" exclaimed Dete angrily. "What could have put it into your head to do that? What made you undress yourself? What do you mean by it?"

"I don't want any clothes," said the child, not showing any sign of repentance for her deed.

"You wretched, thoughtless child! Have you no sense in you at all?" continued Dete, scolding and lamenting. "Who is going all that way down to get them? It's a good half-hour's walk! Peter, bring them for me as quickly as you can, and don't stand there gaping at me, as if you were rooted to the ground!"

"I am already late," answered Peter slowly, without moving.

"Well, you won't get far if you only keep on standing there with your eyes staring out of your head," was Dete's cross reply. "But see, you shall have something nice," and she held out a bright new piece of money that sparkled in the sun. Peter was immediately off down the steep mountainside, taking the shortest cut. In an incredibly short space of time he reached the little heap of clothes and gathered them up under his arm. He was back again so quickly that even Dete was obliged to give him a word of praise as she handed him the promised money. Peter promptly thrust it into his pocket, his face beaming with delight, for it was not often that he was the happy possessor of such riches.

"You may carry the things up for me as far as Uncle's since you are going the same way," went on Dete. She was preparing to continue her climb up the mountainside, which rose in a steep ascent immediately behind the goatherd's hut. Peter willingly undertook to do this. Heidi and the goats went skipping and jumping joyfully beside him.

After a climb of more than three-quarters of an hour they reached the top of the Alm mountain.

Uncle's hut stood on a projection of the rock, exposed indeed to the winds, but where every ray of sun could rest upon it, and a full view could be had of the valley beneath. Behind the hut stood three old fir trees, with long, thick, untrimmed branches. Beyond these rose a further wall of mountain, the lower heights still overgrown with beautiful grass and plants, above which were stonier slopes, covered only with scrub, that led gradually up to the steep, bare, rocky summits.

Against the hut, on the side looking toward the valley, Uncle had put up a seat. Here he was sitting, his pipe in his mouth and his hands on his knees, when the children, the goats, and Dete suddenly climbed into view. Heidi reached the top first. She went straight up to the old man, put out her hand, and said, "Good evening, grandfather."

"So, so, what is the meaning of this?" he asked gruffly, as he gave the child an abrupt shake of the hand, and gazed long and curiously at her from under his bushy eyebrows. Heidi stared steadily back at him in return with unflinching gaze. He was so remarkable looking, with his long beard and thick, gray eyebrows that grew together over his nose and looked just like a bush, that Heidi was unable to take her eyes off him.

Meanwhile Dete had come up, with Peter after

her. The boy stood awhile to watch what was going on.

"I wish you good day, Uncle," said Dete, as she
walked toward him. "I have brought you Tobias
and Adelheid's child. You will hardly recognize her,
for you have never seen her since she was a year old."

"And what has the child to do with me up here?"
asked the old man curtly. "You there," he then
called out to Peter, "be off with your goats, you are
none too early as it is, and take mine with you."

Peter obeyed on the instant and quickly disappeared,
for the old man had given him a look that made him
feel that he did not want to stay any longer.

"The child is here to remain with you," Dete made
answer. "I have, I think, done my duty by her for
these four years, and now it is time for you to do
yours."

"That's it, is it?" said the old man, as he looked at
her with a flash in his eye. "And when the child begins to fret and whine after you, as is the way with
these unreasonable little beings, what am I to do with
her then?"

"That's your affair," retorted Dete. "I know I
had to put up with her without complaint when she
was left on my hands as an infant, and with enough
to do as it was for my mother and myself. Now I
have to go and look after my own earnings, and you

are the next of kin to the child. If you cannot arrange to keep her, do with her as you like. You will have to answer for the result if harm happens to her, though you have hardly need, I should think, to add to the burden already on your conscience."

Now Dete was not quite easy in her own conscience about what she was doing, and consequently was feeling hot and irritable, and said more than she had intended. As she uttered her last words, Uncle rose from his seat. He looked at her in a way that made her draw back a step or two, then flinging out his arm, he said to her in a commanding voice: "Be off with you this instant, and get back as quickly as you can to the place you came from, and do not let me see your face again in a hurry."

Dete did not wait to be told twice. "Good-by to you, then, and to you too, Heidi," she called, as she turned quickly away and started to descend the mountain at a running pace, which she did not slacken till she found herself safely at Dörfli. Again questions came raining down upon her from all sides, for everyone knew Dete. They all knew, too, the particulars of the birth and former history of the child, and they wondered what Dete had done with the little one. From every door and window came voices calling: "Where is the child?" "Where have you left the child, Dete?" and more and more reluctantly Dete made answer, "Up there with Alm-Uncle! With Alm-Uncle, I said."

Then the women began to hurl reproaches at her. First one cried out, "How could you do such a thing!" then another, "To think of leaving a helpless little thing up there," while again and again came the words, "The poor mite! The poor mite!" pursuing her as she went along. Unable at last to bear it any longer, Dete ran as fast as she could until she was beyond the reach of their voices. She was far from happy at the thought of what she had done, for the child had been left in her care by her dying mother. She quieted herself, however, with the idea that she would be better able to do something for Heidi if she was earning plenty of money. It was a relief to her to think that she would soon be far away from all these people who were making such a fuss about the matter, and she rejoiced further still that she was at liberty now to take such a good place.

At Home with Grandfather ⌒

As soon as Dete had disappeared the old man went back to his bench, and there he remained seated, staring at the ground without uttering a sound, while thick curls of smoke floated upward from his pipe. Heidi, meanwhile, was enjoying herself in her new surroundings. She looked about till she found a shed, built against the hut, where the goats were kept; she peeped in, and saw that it was empty. She continued her search and presently came to the fir trees behind the hut. A strong breeze was blowing through them, and there was a rushing and roaring in their topmost branches. Heidi stood still and listened. The sound grew fainter, and she went on again, to the farther corner of the hut, and so around to where her grandfather was sitting. Seeing that he was in exactly the same position as when she left him, she went and placed herself in front of him, and putting her hands behind her back, stood and gazed at him. Her grandfather looked up, but still the little girl continued to stand there without moving.

"What do you want?" he asked.

"I want to see what you have inside the house," said Heidi.

"Come, then!" and the grandfather rose and led the way toward the hut.

"Bring your bundle of clothes in with you," he told her as she was following.

"I shan't want them any more," was her prompt answer.

The old man turned and looked searchingly at the child, whose dark eyes were sparkling in delighted anticipation of what she was going to see inside. "She is certainly not wanting in intelligence," he murmured to himself. "And why shall you not want them any more?" he asked aloud.

"Because I want to go about like the goats with their thin, light legs."

"Well, you may do so if you like," said her grandfather, "but bring the things in; we must put them in the cupboard."

Heidi did as she was told. The old man now opened the door, and Heidi stepped inside after him. She found herself in a good-sized room, which covered the whole ground floor of the hut. A table and a chair were the only furniture. In one corner stood the grandfather's bed, in another was the hearth with a large kettle hanging above it, and on the farther side was the cupboard. The grandfather opened the cupboard door. Inside were his clothes, some hanging

up, others, a couple of shirts, and some socks and
handkerchiefs, lying on a shelf; on a second shelf were
some plates and cups and glasses, and on a higher one
still, a round loaf, smoked meat, and cheese. Everything that Alm-Uncle needed for his food and clothing was kept in this cupboard. Heidi ran quickly
forward and thrust in her bundle of clothes, as far
back behind her grandfather's things as possible, so
that they might not easily be found again. She then
looked carefully round the room, and asked, "Where
am I to sleep, grandfather?"

"Wherever you like," he answered.

Heidi was delighted, and began at once to examine
all the nooks and corners to find out where it would
be pleasantest to sleep. In the corner near her grandfather's bed she saw a short ladder against the wall; up
she climbed and found herself in the hayloft. There
lay a large heap of fresh, sweet-smelling hay. Through
a round window in the wall she could see right down
the valley.

"I shall sleep here, grandfather," she called down
to him. "It's lovely up here. Come up and see how
lovely it is!"

"Oh, I know all about it," he called up.

"I am getting the bed ready now," she called down
again, as she went busily to and fro at her work, "but
I shall want you to bring me up a sheet; you can't
have a bed without a sheet to lie upon."

"All right," said the grandfather. Presently he went to the cupboard, and after rummaging about inside for a few minutes he drew out a long, coarse piece of stuff, which was all he had to do duty for a sheet. He carried it up to the loft, where he found that Heidi had already made a very good bed. She had put an extra heap of hay at one end for a pillow, and had so arranged it that, when she was in bed, she would be able to see comfortably out through the round window.

"That is capital," said her grandfather. "Now we must put on the sheet, but wait a moment first." He went and brought another large bundle of hay to make the bed thicker, so that the child should not feel the hard floor under her. The two together now spread the sheet over the bed, and where it was too long or too broad, Heidi quickly tucked it in under the hay.

"We have forgotten something now, grandfather," she said after a short silence.

"What's that?" he asked.

"A coverlet; when you get into bed, you have to creep in between the sheet and the coverlet."

"Oh, that's the way, is it? But suppose I have no coverlet?" said the old man.

"Well, never mind, grandfather," said Heidi in a consoling tone of voice, "I can take some more hay to put over me," and she was turning quickly to get another armful from the heap, when her grandfather stopped her.

"Wait a moment," he said, and he climbed down the ladder again and went toward his bed. He returned to the loft with a large, thick sack, made of linen, which he threw down, exclaiming, "There, that is better than hay, is it not?"

Heidi began tugging away at the sack with all her little might, in her efforts to get it smooth and straight, but her small hands were not fitted for so heavy a job. Her grandfather came to her assistance, and when they spread it neatly over the bed, it all looked so warm and comfortable that Heidi stood gazing at it in delight. "That is a splendid coverlet," she said, "and the bed looks lovely! I wish it were night, so that I might get inside it at once."

"I think we might have something to eat first," said the grandfather. "What do you think?"

Heidi in the excitement of bedmaking had forgotten everything else, but now when she began to think about food she felt very hungry, for she had had nothing to eat since the piece of bread and little cup of thin coffee that had been her breakfast early that morning before she had started on her long, hot journey. So she answered without hesitation, "Yes, I think so, too."

"Let us go down then, since we both think alike," said the old man, and he followed the child down the ladder. While the old man busied himself at the hearth, toasting a large piece of cheese, Heidi went back and forth to the cupboard. Presently the grandfather got up and came to the table with a jug and the cheese, and there he saw it already neatly laid with the round loaf and two plates and two knives each in its right place. Heidi had taken exact note that morning of all that was in the cupboard, and she knew which things would be wanted for their meal.

"Ah, that's right," said the grandfather. "I am glad to see that you have some ideas of your own, but there is still something missing."

Heidi looked at the jug that was steaming away invitingly, and ran quickly back to the cupboard. At first she could see only a small bowl left on the shelf, but she was not long in perplexity, for a moment later she caught sight of two glasses farther back. Without an instant's loss of time she returned with these and the bowl and put them down on the table.

"Good, I see you know how to set about things; but what will you do for a seat?" The grandfather himself was sitting on the only chair in the room. Heidi flew to the hearth, and dragging the three-legged stool up to the table, sat down upon it.

"Well, you have managed to find a seat for yourself, I see, only rather a low one I am afraid," said the grandfather, "but you would not be tall enough to reach the table even if you sat in my chair. The first thing now, however, is to have something to eat, so come along."

With that he stood up, filled the bowl with milk, and placing it on the chair, pushed it in front of Heidi on her little three-legged stool, so that she now had a table to herself.

When the meal was over, the grandfather went outside to put the goat shed in order. Heidi watched with interest while he first swept it out, and then put fresh straw for the goats to sleep upon. Then he went to the little well shed, cut some long, round sticks, and a small, round board. In this he bored some holes and stuck the sticks into them, and there, as if made by magic, was a three-legged stool. Heidi stood and looked at it, speechless with astonishment.

"What do you think that is?" asked her grandfather.

"It's my stool, I know, because it is such a high one; and it was all made in a minute," said the child, still lost in wonder and admiration.

"She understands what she sees, her eyes are in the right place," the grandfather said.

The time passed happily till evening. Then the wind began to roar louder than ever through the old fir trees. Heidi listened with delight to the sound, and it filled her heart so full of gladness that she skipped and danced around the old trees, as if some

unheard-of joy had come to her. The grandfather
stood and watched her from the shed.

Suddenly a shrill whistle was heard. Heidi paused
in her dancing, and the grandfather came out. Down
from the heights above the goats came springing one
after another, with Peter in their midst. Heidi sprang
forward with a cry of joy and rushed among the
flock, greeting first one and then another of her old
friends of the morning. As they neared the hut the
goats stood still, and then two of their number, two
beautiful, slender animals, one white and one brown,
ran forward to where the grandfather was standing
and began licking his hands. He was holding a little
salt which he always had ready for his goats on their

return home. Peter disappeared with the remainder of his flock. Heidi tenderly stroked the two goats in turn, running first to one side of them and then the other, and jumping about in her glee. "Are they ours, grandfather? Are they both ours? Are you going to put them in the shed? Will they always stay with us?"

Heidi's questions came tumbling out one after the other, so that her grandfather had only time to answer each of them with "Yes, yes." When the goats had finished licking up the salt her grandfather told her to go and get her bowl and the bread.

Heidi obeyed and was soon back again. The grandfather milked the white goat and filled Heidi's basin with the rich, warm milk.

"Now eat your supper," he said, handing her the bowl and a piece of bread, "and then go up to bed. Aunt Dete left another little bundle for you with a nightgown and other small things in it, which you will find at the bottom of the cupboard if you want them. I must go and shut up the goats, so be off and sleep well."

"Good night, grandfather! Good night. What are their names, grandfather, what are their names?" she called after him.

"The white one is named 'Little Swan,' and the brown one 'Little Bear,'" he answered.

"Good night, Little Swan, good night, Little Bear!"

she called again at the top of her voice, for they were already inside the shed. Then she sat down on the seat and began to eat her supper, but the wind was so strong that it almost blew her away, so she finished hastily. Running indoors she climbed up to her bed, where she was soon lying as sweetly and soundly asleep as any young princess on her couch of silk.

The wind grew violent during the night, and the old man got up. "The child will be frightened," he murmured half aloud. He climbed the ladder and went and stood by Heidi's bed.

The moonlight was falling through the round window straight onto Heidi's bed. She lay under the heavy coverlet, her cheeks rosy with sleep, her head peacefully resting on her little round arm. Her baby face wore a happy expression, as though she dreamed of something pleasant. The old man stood looking down on the sleeping child until the moon again disappeared behind the clouds and he could see no more. Then he went back to bed.

Out With the Goats ❧

HEIDI was awakened early the next morning by a loud whistle. The sun was shining through the round window and falling in golden rays on her bed and on the large heap of hay, and as she opened her eyes everything in the loft seemed gleaming with gold.

Heidi felt very happy as she remembered all the many new things that she had seen the day before and which she would see again that day. Above all she thought with delight of the two goats. She jumped out of bed and dressed quickly. Then she climbed down the ladder and ran outside the hut. There stood Peter with his flock of goats. The grandfather was just bringing his two out of the shed to join the others. Heidi ran forward to wish good morning to him and the goats.

"Do you want to go with them up the mountain?" asked her grandfather. Nothing could have pleased Heidi better, and she jumped for joy in answer.

28

While the little girl was bathing at a large tub which stood outside the door, the grandfather went inside the hut, calling to Peter to follow him and bring in his bag. Peter obeyed with astonishment, and laid down the little bag which held his scanty dinner. Inside it the old man put a large piece of bread and an equally large piece of cheese, which made Peter open his eyes, for each was twice the size of the portions which he had for his own dinner.

"There, now there is only the little bowl to add," said the grandfather. "You must milk two bowlfuls for Heidi when she has her dinner, for she is going with you and will remain with you till you return this evening. Take care she does not fall over any of the rocks."

The children started joyfully for the mountain. During the night the wind had blown away all the clouds; the dark-blue sky was spreading overhead, and in its midst was the bright sun shining down on the green slopes of the mountain. Heidi went running hither and thither, shouting with delight, for here were whole patches of delicate red primroses, and there the blue gleam of the lovely gentians, while above them all laughed and nodded the golden rockroses.

Enchanted with all this waving field of brightly colored flowers, Heidi forgot even Peter and the goats. She ran on in front of them off to the side, tempted first one way and then the other, as she caught

sight of some bright spot of glowing red or yellow.
And all the while she was picking whole handfuls of
the flowers which she put into her little apron. Peter
had therefore to be on the alert, and his round eyes,
which did not move very quickly, had more work
than they could well manage, for the goats were as
lively as Heidi. They ran in all directions, and Peter
had to follow, whistling and calling and swinging his
stick to get all the runaways together again.

"Where are you now, Heidi?" he called out somewhat crossly.

"Here," called back a voice from somewhere. Peter could see no one, for Heidi was seated on the
ground at the foot of a small hill thickly overgrown
with sweet-smelling prunella. The whole air seemed
filled with its fragrance, and Heidi thought she had
never smelled anything so delicious. She sat surrounded by the flowers, drawing in deep breaths of
the scented air.

"Come along here!" called Peter again. "You are
not to fall over the rocks; your grandfather gave orders that you were not to do so."

"Where are the rocks?" asked Heidi, without moving.

"Up above, right up above. We have a long way
to go yet, so come along! And on the topmost peak
of all the old bird of prey sits and croaks."

That did it. Heidi immediately sprang to her feet

and ran up to Peter with her apron full of flowers.

"You have enough now," said the boy as they began climbing up again together. "You will stay here forever if you go on picking, and if you gather all the flowers now there will be none for tomorrow."

This last argument seemed a convincing one to Heidi, and moreover her apron was already so full that there was hardly room for another flower. So she now kept with Peter. The goats also became more orderly in their behavior, for they were beginning to smell the plants they loved that grew on the higher slopes, and they climbed up now without pause.

The spot where Peter generally halted for his goats to pasture for the day lay at the foot of the high rocks, which were covered for some distance up by bushes and fir trees, beyond which rose their bare and rugged summits. On one side of the mountain the rock was split into deep clefts. The grandfather had had reason to warn Peter of danger. When they had climbed as far as the halting place, Peter unslung his bag and put it carefully in a little hollow of the ground, for he knew what the wind was like up there and did not want to see his precious belongings sent rolling down the mountain by a sudden gust. Then he threw himself at full length on the warm ground, for he was tired after all his exertions.

Heidi meanwhile unfastened her apron and, rolling

it carefully round the flowers, laid it beside Peter's
bag inside the hollow. She then sat down beside his
outstretched figure and looked about her. The valley
lay far below bathed in the morning sun. In front of
her rose a broad snowfield, high against the dark-blue
sky. To the left was a huge pile of rocks on either
side of which a bare, lofty peak, that seemed to pierce
the blue sky, looked frowningly down upon her.
Peter had fallen asleep, and the goats were climbing
about among the bushes overhead. Heidi had never
felt so happy in her life before. So the time went on,
while to Heidi the mountains seemed to have faces,
and to be looking down at her like old friends. Suddenly she heard a loud, harsh cry overhead, and lifting
her eyes she saw a bird, larger than any she had ever
seen before, with great, spreading wings, wheeling
round and round in wide circles, and uttering a pierc-
ing, croaking kind of sound above her.

"Peter, Peter, wake up!" called out Heidi. "See,
the great bird is there—look, look!"

Peter got up on hearing her call, and together they
sat and watched the bird, which rose higher and higher
in the air till it disappeared behind the gray mountain-
tops.

"Where has it gone to?" asked Heidi.

"Home to its nest," said Peter.

"Is his home right up there? Oh, how nice to be
up so high! Why does he make that noise?"

"Because he can't help it," explained Peter.

"Let us climb up there and see where his nest is," proposed Heidi.

"Oh! Oh! Oh!" exclaimed Peter, his disapproval of Heidi's suggestion becoming more marked with each ejaculation. "Why, even the goats cannot climb so high as that! Besides didn't Uncle say that you were not to fall over the rocks?"

Peter now began suddenly whistling and calling, and one after the other the goats came springing down the rocks until they were all assembled on the green plateau.

Heidi jumped up and ran in and out among them, for it was new to her to see the goats playing together like this, and her delight was beyond words as she joined in their frolics.

Meanwhile Peter had taken the bag out of the hollow and placed the pieces of bread and cheese on the ground in the shape of a square, the larger two on Heidi's side and the smaller on his own, for he knew exactly which were hers and which his. Then he took the little bowl and milked some delicious fresh milk into it from the white goat, and afterward set the bowl in the middle of the square.

He called Heidi to come. "Stop jumping about, it is time for dinner," said Peter.

Heidi sat down. "Is the milk for me?" she asked.

"Yes," replied Peter, "and the two large pieces of

bread and cheese are yours also, and when you have
drunk up that milk, you are to have another bowlful
from the white goat, and then it will be my turn."

Heidi now took up the bowl and drank her milk,
and as soon as she had put it down empty Peter rose
and filled it again for her. Then she broke off a piece
of her bread and held out the remainder, which was
still larger than Peter's own piece, together with the
whole big slice of cheese to her companion, saying,
"You may have that, I have plenty."

Peter looked at Heidi, unable to speak for astonishment. He hesitated a moment for he could not believe that Heidi was in earnest; but she kept on holding
out the bread and cheese, and as Peter still did not
take it, she laid it down on his knees. He saw then
that she really meant it. He seized the food, nodded
his thanks and acceptance of her present, and then
made a more splendid meal than he had known since
he had become a goatherd. Heidi continued to watch
the goats.

"Tell me all their names," she said.

Peter knew these by heart. He began, telling Heidi
the name of each goat in turn as he pointed it out to
her. Heidi listened with great attention, and it was
not long before she could herself distinguish the goats
from one another and could call each by name. There
was the Great Turk with his big horns, who was al-

ways trying to butt the others, so that most of them ran away when they saw him coming and would have nothing to do with their rough companion. Only Greenfinch, the slender, nimble little goat, was brave enough to face him, and would make a rush at him, three or four times in succession, so quickly and skilfully that the Great Turk often stood still quite astounded, not venturing to attack her again. Then there was little White Snowflake, who bleated in such a plaintive and beseeching manner that Heidi already had several times run to it and taken its head in her hands to comfort it.

Just at this moment the pleading cry was heard again. Heidi ran to the little creature and, putting her arms around its neck, asked in a sympathetic voice: "What is it, little Snowflake? Why do you call like that as if in trouble?" The goat pressed closer to Heidi in a confiding way and stopped bleating. Peter called out from where he was sitting, "She cries like that because the old goat is not with her. She was sold at Mayenfeld the day before yesterday, and so will not come up the mountain any more.

"Who is the old goat?" called Heidi back.

"Why, her mother, of course," was the answer.

"Oh, you poor Snowflake!" exclaimed Heidi, clasping the animal gently to her. "But do not cry like that any more. See now, I shall come up here

with you every day, so that you will not be alone any
more, and if you want anything you have only to
come to me."

The young animal rubbed its head contentedly
against Heidi's shoulder, and no longer gave such
plaintive bleats. Heidi had by this time found out a
great many things about the goats. She had decided
that by far the handsomest and best-behaved of the
goats were undoubtedly the two belonging to her
grandfather; they carried themselves with a certain
air of distinction and generally went their own way.
They treated the Great Turk with indifference and
contempt.

"Peter," Heidi said, "the prettiest of all the goats
are Little Swan and Little Bear."

"Yes, I know they are," was the answer. "Alm-
Uncle brushes them down and washes them and gives
them salt, and he has the best shed for them."

All of a sudden Peter leaped to his feet and ran
hastily after the goats. Heidi followed him as fast as
she could, for she was too eager to know what had
happened to stay behind. Peter dashed through the
middle of the flock toward that side of the mountain
where the rocks fell straight down to a great depth
below, and where any thoughtless goat, if it went too
near, might fall over and break all its legs. He had
caught sight of the inquisitive Greenfinch taking leaps
in that direction, and he was only just in time, for the

animal had already sprung to the edge of the abyss.
All Peter could do was to throw himself down and
seize one of her hind legs. Greenfinch, thus taken by
surprise, began bleating furiously, angry at being held
so fast and prevented from continuing her trip of dis-
covery. She struggled to get loose, and tried so obstinately to leap forward that Peter shouted to Heidi
to come and help him, for he could not get up and
was afraid of pulling out the goat's leg altogether.

Heidi had already run up and she saw at once the
danger both Peter and the animal were in. She quickly
gathered a bunch of sweet-smelling leaves, and then,
holding them under Greenfinch's nose, said coaxingly,
"Come, come, Greenfinch, you must not be naughty!
Look, you might fall down there and break your leg,
and that would give you dreadful pain!"

The young animal turned quickly and began contentedly eating the leaves out of Heidi's hand. Meanwhile Peter got on his feet again and with Heidi's help
led the goat back to safety. Peter, now that his goat
was safe, lifted his stick in order to give her a good
beating as punishment, and Greenfinch, seeing what
was coming, shrank back in fear. But Heidi cried
out, "No, no, Peter, you must not strike her! See
how frightened she is!"

"She deserves it," growled Peter, and again lifted
his stick. Then Heidi flung herself against him and
cried indignantly, her dark eyes flashing, "You have

no right to touch her, it will hurt her. Let her alone!"

Peter looked with surprise at the commanding little figure, and reluctantly he let his stick drop. "Well, I will let her off if you will give me some more of your cheese tomorrow," he said, for he was determined to have something to make up to him for his fright.

"You shall have it all, tomorrow and every day. I do not want it," replied Heidi, giving ready consent to his demand. "And I will give you bread as well, a large piece such as you had today. But then you must promise never to beat Greenfinch, or Snowflake, or any of the goats."

"All right," said Peter, "I don't care," which meant that he would agree to the bargain.

The day had crept on toward its close, and now the sun was on the point of sinking out of sight behind the high mountains. Heidi sat down again on the ground and silently gazed at the blue bell-shaped flowers, as they glistened in the evening sun, for a golden light lay on the grass and flowers, and the rocks above were beginning to shine and glow. All at once she sprang to her feet. "Peter! Peter! Everything is on fire! All the rocks are burning, and the great snow mountain and the sky! Oh, look, look! The high rock up there is red with flame! Oh, the beautiful, fiery snow! Stand up, Peter! See, the fire has reached the great bird's nest! Look at the rocks!

Look at the fir trees! Everything, everything is on fire!"

"It is always like that," said Peter composedly, "but it is not really fire."

"What is it?" cried Heidi, as she ran back and forth to look first at one side and then the other, for she felt sure she could not have enough of such a beautiful sight. "What is it, Peter, what is it?" she repeated.

"It gets like that of itself," explained Peter.

"Look, look!" cried Heidi in fresh excitement. "Now they have turned all rose color! Look at that one covered with snow, and that with the high, pointed rocks! What do you call them?"

"Mountains have no names," he answered.

"Oh, how beautiful! Look at the crimson snow! And up there on the rocks there are ever so many roses! Oh! Now they are turning gray! Oh! Oh! Now all the color has died away! It's all gone, Peter." And Heidi sat down on the ground looking as distressed as if everything had really come to an end.

"It will come again tomorrow," said Peter. "Get up, we must go home now." He whistled to his goats and together they all started on their homeward way.

"Is it like that every day? Shall we see it every day when we bring the goats up here?" asked Heidi, as she clambered down the mountain at Peter's side.

"It is like that most days," he replied.

"But will it be like that tomorrow for certain?" Heidi persisted.

"Yes, yes, tomorrow for certain," Peter assured her.

Heidi now felt quite happy again. Her little brain was so full of new impressions and new thoughts that she did not speak any more until they had reached the hut. The grandfather was sitting on a bench under the fir trees.

Heidi ran up to him followed by the white and brown goats, for they knew their own master and stall. Peter called out after her, "Come with me again tomorrow! Good night!" He was anxious for more than one reason that Heidi should go with him the next day.

Heidi ran back quickly and gave Peter her hand, promising to go with him, and then making her way through the goats she once more clasped Snowflake round the neck.

Heidi returned to the fir trees. "Oh, grandfather," she cried, even before she had come up to him, "it was so beautiful. The fire, and the roses on the rocks, and the blue and yellow flowers, and look what I have brought you!" And opening the apron that held her flowers she shook them all out at her grandfather's feet. But how changed the poor flowers were! Heidi hardly knew them again. They looked like dried bits of hay; not a single flower cup stood open.

"Oh, grandfather, what is the matter with them?"

But how changed the poor flowers were!

exclaimed Heidi in shocked surprise. "They were
not like that this morning. Why do they look so
now?"

"They like to stand out there in the sun and not to
be shut up in an apron," said her grandfather.

"Then I will never gather any more. But, grandfather, why did the great bird go on croaking so?"
she asked eagerly.

"Go along now and get into your bath while I go
and get some milk. When we are together at supper
I will tell you all about it."

Heidi obeyed, and when she was sitting on her
high stool before her milk bowl with her grandfather
beside her, she repeated her question.

"He is mocking at the people who live down below
in the villages, because they all go huddling and gos-
siping together, and encourage one another in evil
talking and deeds. He calls out, 'If you would separate and each go your own way and come up here
and live on a height as I do, it would be better for
you!'" There was almost a wildness in the old man's
voice as he spoke, so that Heidi seemed to hear the
croaking of the bird again even more distinctly.

"Why haven't the mountains any names?" Heidi
went on.

"They have names," answered her grandfather,
"and if you can describe them to me I will tell you
what they are called."

Heidi described two of them to him and her grandfather named them both.

Then Heidi went on to give him an account of the whole day, and of how delightful it had all been. She particularly described the fire that had burst out everywhere in the evening.

The grandfather explained to her that it was the sun that did it. "When he says good night to the mountains he throws his most beautiful colors over them, so that they may not forget him before he comes again the next day."

Heidi was delighted with this explanation, and could hardly wait for another day to come so that she might once more climb up with the goats and see how the sun bade good night to the mountains. But she had to go to bed first. All night she slept soundly on her bed of hay, dreaming of shining mountains with red roses all over them, where happy little Snowflake went leaping in and out.

The Visit to Grandmother

D AY after day, almost as soon as the sun was up, Peter appeared with the goats, and the two children climbed up together to the high meadows. Heidi, passing her life thus among the grass and flowers, was burned brown with the sun, and grew strong and healthy. Then the autumn came, and the wind blew louder and stronger, and the grandfather would say sometimes, "Today you must stay at home, Heidi; a sudden gust of the wind would blow a little thing like you over the rocks into the valley below, in a moment."

Whenever Peter heard that he must go alone he looked very unhappy, for he saw nothing but mishaps of all kinds ahead, and did not know how he should bear the long, dull day without Heidi. Then, too, there was the good meal he would miss, and besides that the goats on these days were so naughty and obstinate that he had twice the usual trouble with them. They had grown so accustomed to Heidi's presence that they would run in every direction and refuse to go on when she was not with them.

Heidi was never unhappy, for wherever she was she found something to interest or amuse her. She found her grandfather's hammering and sawing and carpentering very entertaining, and if it should chance to be the day when the large, round, goat's-milk cheese was made she enjoyed beyond measure looking on at this wonderful performance, and watching her grandfather, as with sleeves rolled back, he stirred the great caldron. The thing which attracted her most, however, was the waving and roaring of the three old fir trees on these windy days. She would run away repeatedly from whatever she might be doing, to listen to them, for nothing seemed so strange and wonderful to her as the deep, mysterious sound in the tops of the trees. It was growing colder every day, so Heidi went to the cupboard and got out her shoes and stockings and dress.

One night there was a heavy fall of snow and the next morning the whole mountain was covered with it. There was no Peter that day.

As Heidi and her grandfather were sitting one afternoon on their three-legged stools before the fire there came a great thump at the door followed by several others, and then the door opened. It was Peter, who had made all that noise knocking the snow off his shoes. He was still white all over with it, for he had had to fight his way through deep snowdrifts, and large lumps of snow that had frozen upon him still clung to his clothes.

"Good evening," he said as he came in. He went and placed himself as near the fire as he could, without saying another word, but his whole face was beaming with pleasure at finding himself there. Heidi looked on in astonishment, for Peter was beginning to thaw all over with the warmth, so that he had the appearance of a trickling waterfall.

"Well, General," said the grandfather, "now that you have lost your army you will have to turn to your pen and pencil."

"Why must he turn to his pen and pencil?" asked Heidi immediately, full of curiosity.

"During the winter he must go to school," explained her grandfather, "and learn how to read and write. It's a bit hard, although useful sometimes. Am I not right, General?"

"Yes, indeed," assented Peter.

Heidi's interest was now thoroughly awakened, and she had a hundred questions to put to Peter. He always had great difficulty in putting his thoughts into words, and he found his share of the talk doubly difficult today, for by the time he had an answer ready to one of Heidi's questions she had already put two or three more to him.

The grandfather sat without speaking during this conversation. Now and then a twitch of amusement at the corners of his mouth showed that he was listening.

"Well, now, General, you have been under fire for some time and must want some refreshment. Come and join us," he said at last, and as he spoke he rose and went to get the supper out of the cupboard. As soon as the pleasant meal was over Peter began to get ready for returning home, for it was already growing dark. He had said his "good night" and his thanks, and was just going out, when he turned again and said, "I shall come again next Sunday, this day week, and grandmother sent word that she would like you to come to see her someday."

It was quite a new idea to Heidi that she should go to pay anybody a visit, and she could not get it out of her head. The first thing she said to her grandfather the next day was, "I must go down to see the grandmother today. She will be expecting me."

"The snow is too deep," answered the grandfather.

On the fourth day the whole vast field of snow was hard as ice. Heidi again begged her grandfather to let her go.

The grandfather rose from the table where they were eating dinner and climbed up to the hayloft and brought down the thick sack that was Heidi's coverlet. "Come along!" he said. The child skipped out gleefully after him into the glittering world of snow.

The old fir trees were standing now quite silent,

their branches covered with the white snow, and they
looked so beautiful as they glittered and sparkled in
the sunlight that Heidi jumped for joy at the sight
and kept on calling out, "Come here, come here,
grandfather! The fir trees are all silver and gold!"
The grandfather had gone into the shed and he now
came out dragging a large sled after him. When he
had seen the fir trees he sat down on the sled and lifted
the child on his lap. He wrapped her up in the sack,
so that she might keep warm and comfortable. They
shot down the mountainside with such rapidity that
Heidi thought they were flying through the air like
a bird, and shouted aloud with delight. Suddenly they
came to a standstill, and there they were at Peter's hut.
Her grandfather lifted her out and unwrapped her.
"There you are. Now go in, and when it begins to
grow dark you must start on your way home again."
Then he left her and went up the mountain, pulling
his sled after him.

Heidi opened the door of the hut and found herself
in a tiny, dark kitchen. She opened another door,
and walked into the next room. A table was close to
the door, and as Heidi stepped in she saw a woman
sitting there, putting a patch on a waistcoat which
Heidi recognized at once as Peter's. In the corner sat
an old woman, bent with age, spinning. Heidi was
quite sure this was the grandmother, so she went up
to her and said, "Good day, grandmother, I have come

at last. Did you think I was a long time coming?"

The old woman raised her head and felt for the hand that the child held out. When she had found it, she passed her own over it thoughtfully for a few seconds, and then said, "Are you the child who lives up with Alm-Uncle? Are you Heidi?"

"Yes, yes," answered Heidi. "I have just come down in the sled with grandfather."

"Is it possible! Why, your hands are quite warm! Brigitta, did Alm-Uncle come himself with the child?"

Peter's mother had left her work and risen from the table and now stood looking at Heidi with curiosity, scanning her from head to foot. "I do not know, mother, whether Uncle came himself; it is hardly likely. The child probably makes a mistake."

But Heidi looked steadily at the woman, not at all as if in any uncertainty, and said, "I know quite well who wrapped me up in my bedcover and brought me down in the sled: it was grandfather."

"There was some truth then perhaps in what Peter used to tell us of Alm-Uncle during the summer, when we thought he must be wrong," said grandmother. "But who would ever have believed that such a thing was possible? I did not think the child would live three weeks up there. What is she like, Brigitta?"

Brigitta had so thoroughly examined Heidi on all sides that she was well able to describe her to her mother.

"She has Adelheid's slenderness of figure, but her eyes are dark and her hair curly like her father's and the old man's up there. She takes after both of them, I think."

Heidi meanwhile had not been idle; she had made the round of the room and looked carefully at everything there was to be seen. Suddenly she exclaimed, "Grandmother, one of your shutters is flapping back and forth. Grandfather would put a nail in and make it all right in a minute. It will break one of the panes someday. Look, look, how it keeps on banging!"

"Ah, dear child," said the old woman, "I am not able to see it, but I can hear that and many other things besides the shutter. In the night I often lie awake in fear and trembling, thinking that the whole place will give way and fall and kill us. And there is not a creature to mend anything for us, for Peter does not understand such work."

"But why cannot you see, grandmother, that the shutter is loose? Look, there it goes again. See, that one there!" And Heidi pointed to the particular shutter.

"Alas, child, it is not only the shutter I cannot see. I can see nothing," said the grandmother in a sad voice.

"But if I were to go outside and put back the shutter so that you had more light, then you could see, grandmother?"

"No, no, not even then. No one can make it light for me again."

At these words Heidi broke into loud crying. In her distress she kept sobbing out, "Who can make it light for you again? Can no one do it? Isn't there anyone who can do it?"

The grandmother now tried to comfort the child, but it was not easy to quiet her. Heidi did not often weep, but when she did she could not get over her trouble for a long while. The grandmother tried all means in her power to allay the child's grief, for it went to her heart to hear her sobbing so bitterly. At last she said, "Dear Heidi, you cannot think what a pleasure it is to me to listen to you while you talk. So come and sit beside me and tell me what you do up there, and how grandfather occupies himself. I knew him very well in old days, but for many years now I have heard nothing of him, except through Peter, who never says much."

This was a new and happy idea to Heidi. She quickly dried her tears and said in a comforting voice, "Wait, grandmother, till I have told grandfather everything. He will make it light for you again, I am sure, and will do something so that the house will not fall. He will put everything right for you."

The grandmother was silent, and Heidi began to give her a lively description of her life with the grandfather.

The conversation was all at once interrupted by a heavy thump on the door, and in marched Peter, who stood stock-still, opening his eyes with astonishment, when he caught sight of Heidi. His face beamed with smiles as she called out, "Good evening, Peter."

"What, is the boy back from school already!" exclaimed the grandmother in surprise. "I have not known an afternoon to pass so quickly as this one for years. How is the reading getting on, Peter?"

"Just the same," was Peter's answer.

The old woman gave a little sigh. "Ah, well," she said, "I hoped you would have something different to tell me by this time. You will be twelve years old this February."

"What was it you hoped he would have to tell you?" asked Heidi, interested in all the grandmother said.

"I mean that he should have learned to read by this time," explained the grandmother. "Up there on the shelf is an old prayer book, with beautiful songs in it which I have not heard for a long time and cannot now remember to repeat to myself. I hoped that Peter would soon learn enough to be able to read one of them to me sometimes, but he finds it too difficult."

"I must get a light, it is getting too dark to see," said Peter's mother, who was still busy mending his waistcoat. "I feel, too, as if the afternoon had gone I hardly know how."

Heidi now jumped up from her low chair, and holding out her hand hastily to the grandmother, said, "Good night, grandmother. If it is getting dark I must go home at once," and bidding good-by to Peter and his mother she went toward the door. But the grandmother called out in an anxious voice, "Wait, wait, Heidi; you must not go alone like that, Peter must go with you. Take care of the child, Peter, that she does not fall, and don't let her stand still for fear she should get frozen, do you hear? Has she got something warm to put round her throat?"

"I have not anything to put on," called back Heidi, "but I am sure I shall not be cold," and with that she ran outside and went off at such a pace that Peter had difficulty in overtaking her. The grandmother, still in distress, called out to her daughter, "Run after her, Brigitta. The child will be frozen to death on such a night as this. Take my shawl, run quickly!"

Brigitta ran out. But the children had taken but a few steps before they saw the grandfather coming down to meet them, and in another minute his long strides had brought him to their side.

"That's right, Heidi; you have kept your word," said the grandfather, and then wrapping the sack firmly around her he lifted her in his arms and strode off with her up the mountain.

As soon as Heidi and her grandfather got inside their hut the little girl exclaimed, "Grandfather, tomorrow we must take the hammer and the long nails and fasten grandmother's shutter, and drive lots more nails in other places, for her house shakes and rattles all over."

"We must, must we? Who told you that?" asked her grandfather.

"Nobody told me, but I know it anyway," replied Heidi. "Everything is giving way, and when the grandmother cannot sleep, she lies trembling with fear at the noise, for she thinks that every minute the house will fall down on their heads. Everything now is dark for grandmother and she does not think anyone can make it light for her again, but you will be able to, I am sure, grandfather. Think how dreadful it is for her to be always in the dark, and then to be frightened at what may happen. Nobody can help her but you. Tomorrow we must go and help her; we will, won't we, grandfather?"

The child was clinging to the old man and looking up at him in trustful confidence. The grandfather looked down at Heidi for a while without speaking, and then said, "Yes, Heidi, we will do something to stop the rattling. At least we can do that. We will go down about it tomorrow."

The child went skipping round the room for joy, crying out, "We shall go tomorrow! We shall go tomorrow!"

The grandfather kept his promise. On the following afternoon he brought the sled out again, and as be-

fore, he set Heidi down at the door of the grandmother's hut and said, "Go in now, and when it grows
dark, come out again." Then he put the sack in the
sled and went around the house.

Heidi had hardly opened the door and sprung into
to room when the grandmother, stopping her spinning wheel, called out from her corner, "It's the child
again! Here she comes!" Heidi ran to her, and
seating herself on the little stool close up to the old
woman began to talk to her. All at once there came
the sound of heavy blows against the wall of the hut
and the grandmother gave such a start of alarm that she
nearly upset the spinning wheel. "Ah, the house is
going to fall upon us!" she cried.

But Heidi caught her by the arm, and said sooth-
ingly, "No, no, grandmother, do not be frightened, it
is only grandfather with his hammer. He is mending
up everything, so that you shan't have such fear and
trouble."

"Is it possible! Is it really possible! So the dear
God has not forgotten us!" exclaimed the grandmother. "Go outside, Brigitta, and if it is Alm-Uncle, tell him he must come inside a moment that I may
thank him."

Brigitta went outside and found Alm-Uncle in the
act of fastening some heavy pieces of new wood along
the wall. She stepped up to him and said, "Good
evening, Uncle. Mother and I want to thank you for

doing us such a kind service, and she would like to tell
you herself how grateful she is. I do not know who
else would have done it for us. We shall not forget
your kindness, for I am sure—"

"That will do," said the old man interrupting her.
"I know what you think of Alm-Uncle without your
telling me. Go indoors again, I can find out for myself where the mending is wanted."

Brigitta obeyed on the spot, for Uncle had a way
with him that made few people care to oppose his will.
He went on knocking with his hammer all round the
house, and then mounted the narrow steps to the roof,
and hammered away there, until he had used up all the
nails he had brought with him. Meanwhile it had
been growing dark, and he had hardly come down
from the roof and dragged the sled out from behind
the goat shed when Heidi appeared outside. The
grandfather wrapped her up and carried her up in his
arms as he had done the day before. He had to drag
the sled up the mountain after him, for he feared that
if the child sat in it alone her wrappings would fall off
and she would be nearly if not quite frozen.

So the winter went by. After many years of
joyless life, the blind grandmother had at last found
something to make her happy. She listened for the
little tripping footsteps as soon as day had come, and
when she heard the door open and knew the child was

really there, she would call out, "God be thanked, she has come again!"

Heidi had also grown very fond of the old grandmother, and when at last she knew for certain that no one could make it light for her again, she was overcome with sorrow. The grandmother told her again that she felt the darkness much less when Heidi was with her, and so every fine winter's day the child came traveling down on her sled. The grandfather always took her, and never raised any objection. Indeed he always carried the hammer and other things down on the sled with him and many an afternoon he spent in making the goatherd's cottage sound and tight. It no longer groaned and rattled the whole night through, and the grandmother, who for many winters had not been able to sleep in peace as she did now, said she should never forget what the Uncle had done for her.

Two Visits and What
Came of Them

QUICKLY the winter passed, and still more
quickly the bright, glad summer. Another
winter was drawing to its close. Heidi looked forward with more delight each day to the coming spring,
when the warm south wind would roar through the
fir trees and blow away the snow, and the warm sun
would entice the blue and yellow flowers to show their
heads, and the long days out on the mountain would
come again.

Heidi was now in her eighth year. She had learned
all kinds of useful things from her grandfather. She
knew how to look after the goats as well as anyone.
Little Swan and Little Bear followed her like two
faithful dogs. Twice during the course of this last
winter Peter had brought up a message from the
schoolmaster at Dörfli. He sent word to Alm-Uncle
that he ought to send Heidi to school, but the old
man paid no attention to the message.

The March sun had melted the snow on the mountainside, and the snowdrops were peeping out all over the valley, and the fir trees had shaken off their burden of snow and were again merrily waving their branches in the air.

As Heidi was running about one sunny morning, and had just jumped over the water trough for the tenth time at least, she nearly fell backward into it with fright, for there in front of her, looking gravely at her, stood an old gentleman dressed in black. When he saw how startled she was, he said in a kind voice, "Don't be afraid of me, for I am very fond of children. Shake hands! You must be the Heidi I have heard of. Where is your grandfather?"

"He is sitting by the table, making round wooden spoons," Heidi informed him, as she opened the door.

The stranger was the old village pastor from Dörfli who had been a neighbor of Uncle's when he lived down there, and had known him well. He stepped inside the hut, and going up to the old man, who was bending over his work, said, "Good morning, neighbor."

The grandfather looked up in surprise, and then rising said, "Good morning" in return. He pushed his chair toward the visitor. "If you do not mind a wooden seat there is one for you," he said.

The pastor sat down. "It is a long time since I have seen you, neighbor," he said.

"Or I you," was the answer.

"I have come today to talk over something with you," continued the pastor. "I think you know already what it is that has brought me here," and as he spoke he looked toward the child who was standing at the door, gazing with interest and surprise at the stranger.

"Heidi, go off to the goats," said her grandfather. "You may take them a little salt and stay with them till I come."

Heidi disappeared at once.

"The child ought to have been at school a year ago, and most certainly this last winter," said the pastor. "The schoolmaster sent you word about it, but you gave him no answer. What are you thinking of doing with the child, neighbor?"

"I am thinking of not sending her to school," was the answer.

The visitor, surprised, looked across at the old man, who was sitting on his bench with his arms crossed and a determined expression about his whole person.

"How are you going to let her grow up then?" he asked.

"I am going to let her grow up and be happy among the goats and birds; with them she is safe, and will learn nothing evil."

"But the child is not a goat or a bird, she is a human being. If she learns no evil from these comrades of hers, she will at the same time learn no good. She ought not to grow up in ignorance, and it is time she began her lessons. I have come now that you may have leisure to think over it, and to arrange about it during the summer. This is the last winter that she must be allowed to run wild; next winter she must come regularly to school every day."

"She will do no such thing," said the old man with calm determination.

"Do you mean that by no persuasion can you be brought to see reason, and that you intend to stick obstinately to your decision?" said the pastor, growing somewhat angry.

"Indeed," replied the old man, and there was a tone in his voice that betrayed a growing irritation on his part too. "And does the worthy pastor really mean that he would wish me next winter to send a young child like that some miles down the mountain on ice-cold mornings through storm and snow, and let her return at night when the wind is raging, when even one like ourselves would run a risk of being blown down by it and buried in the snow? And perhaps he may not have forgotten the child's mother, Adelheid? She was a sleepwalker, and had fainting spells. Might not the child be attacked in the same way if obliged to overexert herself? And someone thinks he can come and force me to send her? I will go before all the courts of justice in the country, and then we shall see who will force me to do it!"

"You are quite right, neighbor," said the pastor in a friendly tone of voice. "I understand that it would have been impossible to send the child to school from here. But I see that the child is dear to you. For her sake do what you ought to have done long ago. Come down into Dörfli and live again among your fellow men. What sort of life is this you lead, alone, and with bitter thoughts toward God and man? I should think that you must be half frozen to death in this hut in the winter, and I do not know how the child lives through it!"

"The child has young blood in her veins and a good roof over her head, and let me further tell the pastor, that I know where wood is to be found, and when is the proper time to bring it in. The fire is never out in my hut the whole winter through. I could not go to live in Dörfli. The people despise me and I them; it is therefore best for all of us that we live apart."

"No, no, it is not best for you," said the pastor in an earnest voice. "Believe me, neighbor, the people down there do not dislike you so much as you think. Seek to make your peace with God, pray for forgiveness where you need it, and then come and see how differently people will look upon you, and how happy you may yet be."

The pastor had risen and stood holding out his hand to the old man as he added with renewed earnestness, "I will wager, neighbor, that next winter you will be down among us again, and we shall be good neighbors as of old."

Alm-Uncle gave the pastor his hand and answered him calmly and firmly, "You mean well by me I know, but I say now what I shall continue to say, that I will not send the child to school nor come and live among you."

"Then God help you!" said the pastor, and he turned sadly away and left the hut.

Alm-Uncle was out of humor. When Heidi said as usual that afternoon, "Can we go down to grandmother now?" he answered, "Not today." He did not speak again the whole of that day, and the following morning when Heidi again asked the same question, he replied, "We will see." But before the dinner bowls had been cleared away another visitor arrived, and this time it was Aunt Dete. She had a fine, feathered hat on her head, and a long, trailing skirt to her dress which swept the floor.

The grandfather looked her up and down without uttering a word. But Dete was prepared with an exceedingly pleasant speech and began to once to praise the looks of the child. She told Uncle that she had never lost sight of the idea of taking the child back again, for she well understood that the little one must be much in his way, but she had not been able to do it at first. At last she had heard of something that would be a lucky chance for Heidi. Some im-

mensely wealthy relatives of the people she was serv-
ing, who had one of the most beautiful houses in
Frankfurt, had an only daughter, young and an invalid,
who was always obliged to go about in a wheeled
chair. She was very much alone and had no one to
share her lessons. Her father had spoken to Dete's
mistress about finding a companion for her.

The housekeeper had described the sort of child
they wanted, simple-minded and unspoiled, and not
like most of the children that one saw nowadays.

Dete had thought at once of Heidi and had gone off without delay to see the housekeeper. After Dete had given her a description of Heidi, she had immediately agreed to take her. And no one could tell what good fortune there might be in store for Heidi, if she was once with these people and they took a fancy to her.

"Have you nearly finished what you had to say?" broke in Alm-Uncle, who had allowed her to talk on uninterruptedly so far.

"Ugh!" exclaimed Dete, throwing up her head in disgust. "One would think I had been talking to you about the most ordinary matter. Why, there is not one person in all Prättigau who would not thank God for such news."

"You may take your news to anybody you like, I will have nothing to do with it."

But now Dete leaped up from her seat like a rocket and cried: "You will not send her to church or school, as I was told down in Dörfli. She is my own sister's child and I am responsible for what happens to her. I have everybody in Dörfli on my side. I advise you to think well before bringing it into court, if that is your intention. There are certain things which might be brought up against you which you would not care to hear."

"Be silent!" thundered the Uncle, and his eyes flashed with anger. "Go and be done with you! Never let me see you again with your hat and feather,

and such words on your tongue as you come with
today!" And with that he strode out of the hut.

"You have made grandfather angry," said Heidi,
and her dark eyes had anything but a friendly expression in them as she looked at Dete.

"He will soon be all right again. Come now," said
Dete hurriedly, "and show me where your clothes
are."

"I am not coming," said Heidi.

"Nonesense," exclaimed Dete. Then altering her
tone to one half-coaxing, half-cross, she said, "Come
come, you do not understand any better than your
grandfather. You will have all sorts of good things that
you never dreamed of." Then she went to the cupboard and taking out Heidi's things rolled them up in
a bundle. "Come along now."

"I am not coming," repeated Heidi.

"Don't be so stupid and obstinate, like a goat. Listen to me. You saw that your grandfather was angry
and you heard what he said, that he did not wish ever
to see us again. He wants you now to go away with
me and you must not make him angrier still. You
can't think how nice it is at Frankfurt, and if you do
not like it you can come back again. Your grandfather will be in a good temper again by that time."

"Can I return at once and be back home again here
this evening?" asked Heidi.

"What are you talking about! Come along now!

I tell you that you can come back here when you like. Today we shall go as far as Mayenfeld, and early tomorrow we shall start in the train, and that will bring you home again in no time when you wish it, for it goes as fast as the wind."

Dete put the bundle under her arm and took the child by the hand, and so they went down the mountain together.

On the way they met Peter, who had stolen a holiday from school that day. He thought it a far better employment to wander about a bit and look for stout sticks which might be wanted someday. He had evidently been well rewarded that day for his labors, for he was carrying an immense bundle of long, thick hazel sticks on his shoulders. He stood still and stared at the two approaching figures. As they came up to him, he exclaimed, "Where are you going, Heidi?"

"I am only just going over to Frankfurt for a little visit with Dete," she replied. "But I must first run in to grandmother, she will be expecting me."

"No, no, you must not stop to talk; it is already too late," said Dete, holding fast to Heidi's hand as she struggled to get away. "You may go in when you come back. Come along now."

Peter ran into the hut and banged against the table with his bundle of sticks with such violence that everything in the room shook, and his grandmother leaped up with a cry of alarm from her spinning wheel.

"What is the matter? What is the matter?" cried the frightened old woman.

"She is taking Heidi away," Peter said crossly.

"Who? Who? Where to, Peter, where to?" asked the grandmother, growing still more agitated, but even as she spoke she guessed what had happened, for Brigitta had told her shortly before that she had seen Dete going up to Alm-Uncle. The old woman rose hastily and with trembling hands opened the window and called out beseechingly, "Dete, Dete, do not take the child away from us! Do not take her away!"

When Heidi heard that she struggled to get free, crying, "Grandmother is calling, I must go to her."

But Dete had no intention of letting the child go. She told her that when she wanted to return home she could do so at once, and then she could take something she liked back to grandmother. This was a new idea to Heidi, and it pleased her so much that Dete had no longer any difficulty in getting her along.

After a few minutes' silence, Heidi asked, "What could I take back to her?"

"We must think of something nice," answered Dete. "She would enjoy a soft roll of white bread, for now she is old she can hardly eat the hard, black bread."

"No, she always gives it back to Peter, telling him it is too hard. I have seen her do it myself," agreed Heidi. "Do let us make haste, for then perhaps we can get back soon from Frankfurt, and I shall be able to give her the white bread today."

Heidi started running so fast that Dete with the bundle under her arm could scarcely keep up with her. But she was glad, nevertheless, to get along so quickly. She went on straight ahead through Dörfli, holding Heidi tightly by the hand, so that all the people might see that it was on the child's account she was hurrying along at such a rate. To all their questions and remarks she made answer as she passed, "I can't stop now, as you see. I must make haste with the child for we have yet some way to go."

From that day Alm-Uncle looked fiercer and more forbidding than ever when he came down and passed through Dörfli. He spoke to no one, and looked like such an ogre with his thick, frowning eyebrows drawn together as he came along with his pack of cheeses on his back and his immense stick in his hand, that the women would call to their little ones, "Take care! Get out of Alm-Uncle's way or he may hurt you!"

The old man took no notice of anybody as he strode through the village on his way to the valley below, where he sold his cheeses and bought what bread and meat he wanted for himself. After he had passed, the villagers all crowded together looking after him, and each had something to say about him; how much wilder he looked than usual and how now he would not even respond to anybody's greeting. They all agreed that it was a great mercy the child had gotten away from him. They had all noticed how the child had hurried along as if afraid that her grandfather might be following to take her back. Only the blind grandmother would have nothing to say against him. She told those who came to her to bring her work, or take away what she had spun, how kind and thoughtful he had been with the child, how good to her and her daughter, and how many afternoons he had spent mending the house which, but for his help, would certainly by this time have fallen down over their heads. All this was repeated down in Dörfli, but most of the people did not believe it.

The days were sad again now for the old blind woman, and not one passed but what she would murmur complainingly: "Alas! All our happiness and pleasure have gone with the child, and now the days are so long and dreary! Pray God that Heidi comes again before I die!"

A New Chapter ℘
About New Things

In her home at Frankfurt, Clara, the little daughter
of Mr. Sesemann, was sitting in the rolling chair
in which she spent her whole day. She was wheeled
in it from room to room as she wished. Just now she
was in what was known as the study.

Clara's little face was thin and pale. At this moment her soft, blue eyes were fixed on the clock,
which seemed to her to go very slowly this day. With
a slight accent of impatience, which was very rare
with her, she asked, "Isn't it time yet, Miss Rottenmeier?"

This lady was sitting up very straight at a small
work table, busy with her embroidery. She had on a
mysterious-looking, loose garment, with a large collar
or shoulder cape that gave to her appearance a certain solemnity which was increased by a very high
dome-shaped headdress. For many years past, since
the mistress of the house had died, Miss Rottenmeier
had been the housekeeper. Mr. Sesemann was often

away from home, and he left her in sole charge. The only condition he made was that his little daughter should have a voice in all matters, and that nothing should be done against her wish.

As Clara was putting her impatient question for the second time, Dete and Heidi arrived at the front door. Dete inquired of the coachman, who had just descended from his box, if it was too late to see Miss Rottenmeier.

"That's not my business," grumbled the coachman. "Ring the bell in the hall for Sebastian."

Dete did so, and Sebastian came downstairs. He looked astonished when he saw her, opening his eyes till they were nearly as big as the large, round buttons on his coat.

"Is it too late for me to see Miss Rottenmeier?" Dete asked again.

"That's not my business," answered the man. "Ring that other bell for the maid Tinette." Without troubling himself any further Sebastian disappeared.

Dete rang again. This time Tinette appeared.

"What is it?" she called from the top of the stairs. Dete repeated her question. Tinette disappeared, but soon came back and called down to Dete, "Come up, she is expecting you."

Dete and Heidi went upstairs and into the study. Dete remained standing politely near the door, still holding Heidi tightly by the hand.

Miss Rottenmeier rose slowly and went up to the new little companion for the daughter of the house. She did not seem very pleased with the child's appearance. Heidi was dressed in her plain little woolen frock, and her hat was an old straw one bent out of shape. The child looked innocently out from under it, gazing with unconcealed astonishment at the lady's towering headdress.

"What is your name?" asked Miss Rottenmeier.

"Heidi," the child answered in a clear, ringing voice.

"What? What? That's no Christian name for a child; you were not christened that. What name did they give you when you were baptized?" demanded Miss Rottenmeier.

"I do not remember," replied Heidi.

"What a way to answer!" said the lady, shaking her head. "Dete, is the child a simpleton or only saucy?"

"If the lady will allow me, I will speak for the child for she is very unaccustomed to strangers," said Dete, giving Heidi a poke for making such an unsuitable answer. "This is the first she has been in a gentleman's house and she does not know good manners. I hope the lady will excuse her. She was christened 'Adelheid' after her mother, my sister, who is now dead."

"Well, that's a name that one can pronounce,"

remarked Miss Rottenmeier. "But I must tell you, Dete, that I am astonished to see so young a child. I told you that I wanted a companion of the same age as the young lady of the house, one who could share her lessons, and all her other occupations. Miss Clara is now over twelve; what age is this child?"

"I am sorry," said Dete, "but I myself had lost count of her exact age. I cannot say precisely, but I think she is about ten."

"Grandfather told me I was eight," put in Heidi. Dete gave her another poke, but the child had not the least idea why and was not at all confused.

"What—only eight!" cried Miss Rottenmeier angrily. "Four years too young! Of what use is such a child! And what have you learned? What books did you have to learn from?"

"None," said Heidi.

"How? What? How then did you learn to read?" demanded the lady.

"I have never learned to read, or Peter either," Heidi informed her.

"Mercy upon us! You do not know how to read! Is it really so?" exclaimed Miss Rottenmeier, greatly horrified. "Is it possible—not able to read? What have you learned then?"

"Nothing," said Heidi with unflinching truthfulness.

"Young woman," said the lady to Dete, when she

had paused for a minute or two to recover from her shock, "this is not at all the sort of companion you led me to expect. How could you think of bringing me a child like this?"

But Dete was not to be put down so easily, and answered warmly, "I am sorry, but the child is exactly what I thought you wanted. You said you wished a child unlike all other children, and I thought this child seemed as if made for the place. But I must go now, for my mistress will be waiting for me. I will come again soon and see how the child is getting on." And with a bow Dete quickly left the room and ran downstairs.

Miss Rottenmeier ran after her. If the child was to stay she had many things yet to ask about her.

Heidi remained by the door where she had been standing since she first came in. Clara had looked on during the interview without speaking. Now she beckoned to Heidi and said, "Come here!"

Heidi went up to her.

"Would you rather be called 'Heidi' or 'Adelheid'?" asked Clara.

"I am never called anything but 'Heidi,' " was the child's prompt answer.

"Then I shall always call you by that name," said Clara. "It suits you. I have never heard it before, but neither have I ever seen a child like you before. Have you always had that short curly hair?"

"Yes, I think so," said Heidi.

"Are you pleased to come to Frankfurt?" went on Clara.

"No, but I shall go home again tomorrow and take grandmother a white loaf," explained Heidi.

"Well, you are a funny child!" exclaimed Clara. "You were expressly sent for to come stay with me and share my lessons. There will be some fun about them now, since you cannot read. Often they are dreadfully dull, and I think the morning will never pass away. You know, my tutor comes every morning at about ten o'clock, and then we go on with lessons till two, and it does seem such a long time. I often want to yawn, but I am obliged to stop myself, for if Miss Rottenmeier sees me yawning she runs off at once and gets the cod-liver oil and says I must have a dose, because I am getting weak again. But now it will be much more amusing, for I shall be able to lie and listen while you learn to read."

Heidi shook her head doubtfully when she heard of learning to read.

"Oh, nonsense, Heidi, of course you must learn to read. Everybody must, and my tutor is very kind, and never cross, and he will explain everything to you."

Miss Rottenmeier now came back into the room. She had not been able to overtake Dete, and was evidently very much put out. She felt responsible for

Heidi's coming and she did not know how to undo the mischief.

Presently Sebastian flung open the folding doors leading into the dining room. He then went up to Clara's chair to wheel her into the next room. Heidi stood staring at him. Seeing her eyes fixed upon him, he suddenly growled out, "Well, what is there in me to stare at like that?"

"You look so much like Peter," answered Heidi.

Sebastian wheeled Clara into the dining room and helped her to her place. Miss Rottenmeier took the seat beside her and made a sign to Heidi to take the one opposite. They were the only three at table, and as they sat far apart there was plenty of room for Sebastian to hand his dishes. Beside Heidi's plate lay a white roll, and her eyes lighted up with pleasure as she saw it. The resemblance which Heidi had noticed had evidently awakened in her a feeling of confidence toward Sebastian, for she sat as still as a mouse and without moving until he came up to her side and handed her the dish of fish. Then she looked at the roll and asked, "May I have it?"

Sebastian nodded, throwing a side glance at Miss Rottenmeier to see what effect this request would have upon her. Heidi immediately seized the roll and put it in her pocket. Sebastian's face became convulsed. He was overcome with inward laughter, but he knew his place too well to laugh aloud. Heidi looked wonderingly at him for a minute or two, and then said, "Am I to eat some of that, too?" Sebastian nodded again. "Give me some then," she said, looking calmly at her plate. At this Sebastian's command of his countenance became doubtful, and the dish began to tremble suspiciously in his hands.

"You may put the dish on the table and come back presently," said Miss Rottenmeier with a severe expression on her face. Sebastian disappeared immediately. "As for you, Adelheid, I see I shall have to teach you the first rules of behavior," continued the housekeeper with a sigh. "I will begin by explaining to you how you are to conduct yourself at table," and she went on to give Heidi minute instructions as to all she was to do. "And now," she continued, "I must make you particularly understand that you are not to speak to Sebastian at table, or at any other time, unless you have an order to give him, or a necessary question to put to him. Then you are not to address him as if he were a relative. Never let me hear you speak to him in that way again. It is the same with Tinette, and for myself you are to address me as you hear others doing. Clara must decide herself what you are to call her."

"Why, 'Clara,' of course," said that little girl at once. The housekeeper went on with a long list of rules as to general behavior, getting up and going to bed, going in and out of the room, shutting the doors, keeping everything neat. As she talked Heidi's eyes gradually closed, for she had been up before five o'clock that morning and had had a long journey. She learned back in her chair and fell fast asleep. When Miss Rottenmeier had at last come to the end of her sermonizing she said, "Now remember what I have said, Adelheid! Have you understood it all?"

"Heidi has been asleep for ever so long," said Clara, her face rippling all over with amusement. She had not had such an entertaining dinner for a long time.

"It is really unendurable what one has to go through with this child," exclaimed Miss Rottenmeier, in great indignation, and she rang the bell so violently that Tinette and Sebastian both came running in, nearly tumbling over one another. But no noise was sufficient to wake Heidi, and it was with difficulty they could rouse her sufficiently to get her to her bedroom.

Miss Rotteneier Spends ꧂
an Uncomfortable Day

W HEN Heidi awakened on her first morning in Frankfurt she could not think where she was. She rubbed her eyes and looked about her. She was sitting up in a high, white bed, on one side of a large, wide room, into which the light was falling through very, very long white curtains. All at once she remembered that she was in Frankfurt. Everything that had happened the day before came back to her. Hastily she jumped out of bed.

When she was dressed she ran first to one window and then another. She wanted to see the sky and country outside. She felt like a bird in a cage behind those great curtains. They were too heavy for her to put aside, so she crept underneath them to get to the window. But the windows were so high that she could just get her head above the sill to peer out. Even then she could not see what she longed for. Heidi felt quite frightened. She ran back and forth trying to open first one and then the other of the windows. She felt she could not bear to see nothing but walls and windows. Somewhere outside there must be the green grass, and the last unmelted snows on the mountain slopes, which Heidi so longed to see.

At that moment a knock came on the door, and Tinette put her head inside and said, "Breakfast is ready." Heidi had no idea what an invitation so worded meant, and Tinette's face did not encourage any questioning on Heidi's part. She drew the little stool out from under the table, put it in the corner and sat down upon it, and there silently awaited what would happen next. In a few minutes Miss Rottenmeier appeared. She seemed very much put out again.

"What is the matter with you, Adelheid?" she said severely. "Don't you understand what breakfast is? Come along at once!"

Heidi had no difficulty in understanding now, and followed at once. Clara had been some time at the breakfast table and she gave Heidi a kindly greeting. Her face was considerably more cheerful than usual, for she expected all kinds of new things to happen again that day. After breakfast the two children went into the study.

As soon as they were alone, Heidi asked, "How can you see out from here, and look right down on the ground?"

"You must open the window and look out," replied Clara, amused.

"But the windows won't open," said Heidi sadly.

"Yes, they will," Clara assured her. "You cannot open them, nor I either, but when you see Sebastian you can ask him to open one."

It was a great relief to Heidi to know that the windows could be opened and that one could look out, for she still felt as if she were shut up in prison. Clara began to ask her questions about her home, and Heidi was delighted to tell her all about the mountain and the goats, and the flowery meadows which were so dear to her.

Meanwhile the tutor had arrived. Miss Rottenmeier, however, did not bring him straight into the study, but drew him first aside into the dining room, where she poured forth her troubles and explained to him the awkward position in which she was placed. She wanted him to help her get rid of Heidi, but the tutor was an extremely cautious man and would not say much.

When Miss Rottenmeier saw that he was not ready to support her, and evidently quite ready to undertake teaching Heidi the alphabet, she opened the study door and quickly shut it again as soon as he had gone through. She walked up and down the dining room, thinking over in her own mind how the servants were to be told to address Adelheid. Suddenly the sound of a frightful crash was heard in the study, followed by frantic cries for Sebastian. She rushed into the room. There on the floor in a confused heap lay

books, exercise books, inkstand, and other articles
with the tablecloth on the top. From beneath the pile
a dark stream of ink was flowing across the floor.
Heidi had disappeared.

"Here's a state of things!" exclaimed Miss Rottenmeier, wringing her hands. "Tablecloth, books,
work-basket, everything, lying in the ink! It was that
unfortunate child I suppose."

The tutor was standing looking down at the havoc
in distress. Clara appeared to find pleasure in such an
unusual event and in watching the results.

"Yes, Heidi did it," she explained, "but quite by
accident. She must on no account be punished. She
jumped up in such violent haste to get away that she
dragged the tablecloth along with her, and so every
thing went over. There were a number of carriages
passing; that is why she rushed off like that."

"Is it not as I said? She has not the smallest notion
about anything! Not the slightest idea that she ought
to sit still and listen while her lessons are going on.
But where is the child who has caused all this trouble?
Surely she has not run away! What would Mr. Sesemann say to me?" She ran out of the room and down
the stairs. There, at the bottom, standing in the open
doorway, was Heidi, looking in amazement up and
down the street.

"What are you doing? What are you thinking of
to run away like that?" called Miss Rottenmeier.

"I heard the sound of the fir trees, but I cannot see where they are, and now I cannot hear them any more," answered Heidi, looking disappointedly up the street.

"Fir trees! Do you suppose we are in a wood? What ridiculous ideas are these? Come upstairs and see the mischief you have done!"

Heidi turned and followed Miss Rottenmeier upstairs. She was quite astonished to see the disaster she had caused, for in her joy and haste to get to the fir trees she had been unaware of having dragged everything after her.

"I excuse you for doing this because it is the first time, but do not let me hear of your doing it a second time," said Miss Rottenmeier pointing to the floor. "During your lesson time you are to sit still and listen. If you cannot do this I shall have to tie you to your chair. Do you understand?"

"Yes," replied Heidi, "but I will not move again."

When the servants had straightened the room it was too late for any more lessons. There had been no time for yawning this morning.

In the afternoon while Clara was resting, Heidi was left to her own devices. She took her stand in the hall in front of the dining room door in order to stop Sebastian when he came up from the kitchen with the silver. As he reached the top stair Heidi went up to him. "I want to ask you something," she said.

"What was it little miss wished to ask?" said Sebastian as he went on into the dining room to put away his silver.

"How can a window be opened?"

"Why, like that!" and Sebastian flung up one of the large windows.

Heidi ran to it, but she was not tall enough to see out, for her head only reached to the sill.

"There, now miss can look out and see what is going on below," said Sebastian as he brought her a high wooden stool to stand on.

Heidi climbed up, and at last, as she thought, was going to see what she had been longing for. But she drew back her head with a look of great disappointment on her face.

"Why, there is nothing outside but the stony streets," she said mournfully. "If I went right around to the other side of the house what should I see there, Sebastian?"

"Nothing but what you see here," he told her.

"Then where can I go to see away over the whole valley?"

"You would have to climb to the top of a high tower, like that one over there with the gold ball above it. From there you can see away ever so far."

Heidi climbed down quickly from her stool, ran to the door, down the steps, and out into the street. She could no longer see the tower, however. She hurried along street after street, but still she did not come to the tower. At one of the street corners she saw a boy standing, carrying a hand organ on his back and a funny-looking animal on his arm. Heidi ran up to him and said, "Where is the tower with the gold ball on the top?"

"I don't know," the boy answered.

"Whom can I ask to show me?" she asked again.

"I don't know."

"Do you know any other church with a high tower?"

"Yes, I know one."

"Come then and show it to me."

"Show me first what you will give me for it," and the boy held out his hand as he spoke. Heidi had nothing but a card with a garland of beautiful red roses painted on it. Clara had only that morning made her a present of it—but then, to look down into the valley and see all the lovely green slopes!

The boy refused it, however, when she offered it to him.

"What would you like then?" asked Heidi, not sorry to put the card back in her pocket.

"Money."

"I have none, but Clara has. How much do you want?"

"Five cents."

"Come along then."

They started off together along the street, and on the way Heidi asked her companion what he was carrying on his back. It was a hand organ, he told her, which played beautiful music when he turned the handle. All at once they found themselves in front of an old church with a high tower. The boy stood still, and said, "There it is."

Heidi caught sight of a bell and immediately pulled it with all her might. The boy promised to wait and show her the way home, for another five cents.

They heard the key turning inside, and then someone pulled open the heavy, creaking door. An old man came out and at first looked in surprise and then in anger at the children. "What do you mean by ringing me down?" he scolded. "Can't you read what is written over the bell. 'For those who wish to go up to the tower'?"

The boy said nothing, but pointed his finger at Heidi. She said, "But I do want to go up the tower."

"What do you want up there?" said the old man. "Has somebody sent you?"

"No," replied Heidi, "I only wanted to go up that I might look down."

"Get along home with you and don't try this trick on me again, or you may not come off so easily a second time." He turned and was about to shut the door, but Heidi took hold of his coat and said beseechingly, "Let me go up, just once."

He looked round, and his mood changed as he saw her pleading eyes. He took hold of her hand and said kindly, "Well, if you really wish it so much, I will take you."

They climbed up many steps, which became smaller and smaller as they neared the top, and at last they came to one very narrow one, and there they were at the end of their climb. The old man lifted Heidi up so that she might look out of the open window.

"There, now you can look down," he said.

Heidi saw beneath her a sea of roofs, towers, and chimneys. She quickly drew back her head and said in a sad, disappointed voice, "It is not at all what I thought."

"You see now, a child like you does not understand anything about a view! Come along down and don't you go ringing my bell again!"

He lifted her down and went on before her down the narrow stairway. Near the tower keeper's room sat a big, gray cat guarding a basket. To Heidi's delight the old man opened the basket and showed her the kittens that were playing about in it.

"Oh, the sweet little things! The darling kittens!" Heidi exclaimed, as she jumped from side to side of the basket.

"Would you like to have one?" said the old man, who enjoyed watching the child's pleasure.

"For myself, to keep?" said Heidi excitedly, who

could hardly believe such happiness was to be hers.

"Yes, of course, more than one if you like. You may take away the whole lot if you have room for them." The old man was only too glad to think he could get rid of his kittens without more trouble.

Heidi could hardly contain herself for joy. There would be plenty of room for them in the large house, and how astonished and delighted Clara would be when she saw the sweet little kittens.

"But how can I take them with me?" asked Heidi.

"I will take them for you, if you tell me where," said the old man.

"To Mr. Sesemann's, the big house where there is a gold dog's head on the door, with a ring in its mouth," explained Heidi.

"I know the house," the old man said. "When shall I bring them, and whom shall I ask for? You are not one of the family, I am sure."

"No, but Clara will be so delighted when I take her the kittens."

Heidi could hardly tear herself away from the kittens, so the man let her take two with her, one in each pocket.

When she got downstairs she found the boy still sitting outside on the steps.

"Which is the way to Mr. Sesemann's house?" she asked.

"I don't know," was the answer.

Heidi began a description of the front door and the steps and the windows, but the boy only shook his head, and was not any the wiser.

"Well, look here," said Heidi. "From one window you can see a very, very large, gray house, and the roof runs like this." She drew a zigzag line in the air with her forefinger.

The boy was evidently in the habit of guiding himself by similar landmarks. He jumped up at once and ran off with Heidi after him. In a very short time they had reached the door with the large dog's head for a knocker. Heidi rang the bell. Sebastian opened the door almost at once. "Make haste! Make haste," he cried in a hurried voice, when he saw Heidi.

Heidi ran in hastily and Sebastian shut the door after her, leaving the boy, whom he had not noticed, standing in wonder on the steps.

"Make haste, little miss," said Sebastian again. "Go straight into the dining room. They are already at table. Miss Rottenmeier looks like a loaded cannon. What could make the little miss run off like that?"

Heidi walked into the room. The housekeeper did not look up and Clara did not speak. There was an uncomfortable silence. Sebastian pushed Heidi's chair up for her. When she was seated Miss Rottenmeier, with a severe countenance, sternly and solemnly addressed her.

"I will speak with you afterward, Adelheid. I will

only say now that you behaved in a most unmannerly and wrong way by running out of the house as you did, without asking permission, without anyone's knowing a word about it. And then to go wandering about till this hour! I never heard of such behavior before."

"Miaow!" came the answer back.

This was too much for the lady's temper. Raising her voice she exclaimed, "You dare, Adelheid, after your bad behavior, to answer me as if it were a joke?"

"I did not—" began Heidi. "Miaow! Miaow!"

Sebastian almost dropped his dish and rushed out of the room.

"That will do," Miss Rottenmeier tried to say, but her voice was half stifled with anger. "Get up and leave the room."

Heidi stood up, frightened, and again made an attempt to explain. "I really did not—" "Miaow! Miaow! Miaow!"

"But, Heidi," now put in Clara, "when you see that it makes Miss Rottenmeier angry, why do you keep on saying 'Miaow'?"

"It isn't I, it's the kittens," Heidi was at last given time to say.

"How! What! Kittens!" shrieked Miss Rottenmeier. "Sebastian! Tinette! Find the horrid little things! Take them away!" And she rose and fled into the study and locked the door, to make sure that she was safe from the kittens, which to her were the most horrible things in the world.

Sebastian promised to make a bed in a basket for the kittens and to take care of them.

It was almost bedtime before Miss Rottenmeier ventured to open the door a crack and call through, "Have you taken those dreadful little animals away, Sebastian?"

Sebastian quickly and quietly caught up the kittens from Clara's lap. Assuring the housekeeper that they were gone, he disappeared with them.

The scolding which Miss Rottenmeier had intended to give Heidi was put off till the following day. She felt too exhausted now after all the emotions she had gone through of irritation, anger, and fright, of which Heidi had unintentionally been the cause. She retired without speaking. Clara and Heidi followed, happy at knowing that the kittens were lying in a comfortable bed.

There Is Great Commotion 〜
in the Large House

SEBASTIAN had just shown the tutor into the study on the following morning when there came such a very loud ring at the bell that Sebastian thought it was Mr. Sesemann. He pulled open the door. There in front of him stood a ragged little boy carrying a hand organ on his back.

"What's the meaning of this?" said Sebastian angrily. "I'll teach you to ring bells like that! What do you want here?"

"I want to see Clara," the boy answered.

"You dirty, good-for-nothing little rascal, can't you be polite enough to say 'Miss Clara'? What do you want with her?" demanded Sebastian roughly.

"She owes me ten cents," explained the boy.

"You must be out of your mind! And how do you know that any young lady of that name lives here?"

"She owes me five cents for showing her the way there, and five cents for showing her the way back."

"What a pack of lies you are telling! The young

lady never goes out. She cannot even walk. Be off and get back to where you came from, before I have to help you along."

But the boy was not to be frightened away. He stood still, and said in a determined voice, "But I saw her in the street. I can describe her to you. She has short, curly black hair, black eyes, and wears a brown dress, and does not talk quite as we do."

"Oho!" thought Sebastian, laughing to himself, "the little miss has evidently been up to more mischief." Then, drawing the boy inside he said aloud, "I understand now. Come with me and wait outside the door till I tell you to go in. Be sure you begin playing your organ the instant you get inside the room."

Sebastian knocked at the study door, and a voice said, "Come in."

"There is a boy outside who says he must speak to Miss Clara herself," Sebastian announced.

Clara was delighted at such an extraordinary and unexpected message.

"Let him come in at once," replied Clara. "He must come in, must he not," she added, turning to her tutor, "if he wishes so particularly to see me."

The boy was already inside the room, and according to Sebastian's directions immediately began to play his organ. Miss Rottenmeier was in the next room when she heard the music. She rushed into the study and stopped aghast at sight of the boy with his organ.

"Stop! Stop at once!" she screamed. But her voice was drowned by the music. She was making a dash for the boy, when she saw something on the ground crawling toward her feet—a dreadful, dark object—a tortoise! At this sight she jumped higher than she had for many long years, shrieking with all her might, "Sebastian! Sebastian!"

The organ player suddenly stopped, for this time her voice had risen louder than the music. Sebastian was standing outside bent double with laughter, for he had been peeping to see what was going on. By the time he entered the room Miss Rottenmeier had sunk into a chair.

"Take them all out, boy and animal! Get them away at once!" she commanded him.

Sebastian pulled the boy away, and when they were outside he put something into his hand. "There is ten cents from Miss Clara, and another ten cents for the music. You did it all quite right!"

Quietness reigned again in the study, and lessons began once more. Miss Rottenmeier now took up her station in order to prevent anything further happening.

But soon another knock came on the door, and Sebastian again stepped in, this time with a large, covered basket for Miss Clara.

"I think the lessons had better be finished first be-

Sebastian waited to get over his laughter before entering.

fore the basket is unpacked," said Miss Rottenmeier.

Clara could not imagine what was in it, and cast longing glances toward it. In the middle of one of her declensions she suddenly broke off and said to the tutor, "Mayn't I give just one peep inside to see what is in it before I go on?"

"On some considerations I am for it, on others against it," he began in answer; "for it, on the ground that if your whole attention is directed to the basket —"but the speech remained unfinished. The cover of the basket was loose, and at this moment one, two, three, and then two more, and again more kittens came suddenly tumbling out on the floor. They raced about the room in every direction, and with such indescribable rapidity that it seemed as if the whole room were full of them. They jumped over the tutor's boots, bit at his trousers, climbed up Miss Rottenmeir's dress, rolled about her feet, sprang up on Clara's chair, scratching, scrambling, and miaowing. It was a sad scene of confusion.

Clara, pleased with their gambols, kept on exclaiming, "Oh, the dear little things! How pretty they are! Look, Heidi, at this one. Look, look, at that one over there!" And Heidi in her delight kept running after them first into one corner and then into another. The tutor stood up by the table not knowing what to do, lifting first his right foot and then his left to get away from the scrambling, scratching kittens.

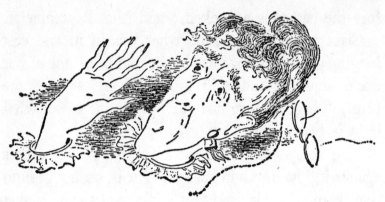

Miss Rottenmeier was unable at first to speak at all, so overcome was she with horror. She did not dare rise from her chair for fear that all the dreadful little animals should jump upon her at once. At last she found voice to call loudly, "Tinette! Tinette! Sebastian! Sebastian!"

They came in answer to her summons and gathered up the kittens. By degrees they got them all inside the basket again and then carried them off to put with the other two.

Today again there had been no opportunity for yawning.

Miss Rottenmeier soon discovered that Heidi was responsible for the morning's happenings.

"Adelheid," she said, severely, "I know of only one punishment for you. I shall put you in a dark cellar with the rats and black beetles."

Heidi listened in silence and surprise. She had never seen a cellar such as Miss Rottenmeier described.

The place known at her grandfather's as the cellar, where the fresh-made cheeses and the new milk were kept, was a pleasant and inviting place. Neither did she know at all what rats and black beetles were like.

But Clara cried in great distress. "No, no, Miss Rottenmeier, you must wait till papa comes. He has written to say that he will soon be home, and then I will tell him everything, and he will say what is to be done with Heidi."

Miss Rottenmeier could not do anything against the superior authority. She answered with some displeasure, "As you will, Clara, but I too shall have something to say to Mr. Sesemann."

Two days now went by without further disturbance. Clara had grown much more cheerful since Heidi had come. She no longer found time hanging heavy during the lesson hours, for Heidi was continually making a diversion of some kind or other. She jumbled all her letters up together and seemed quite unable to learn them.

In the late afternoon Heidi always sat with Clara. She entertained the little invalid with long descriptions of the mountain and of her life upon it, and the burning longing to return would become so overpowering that she always finished with the words, "Now I must go home! Tomorrow I must really go!"

But Clara would try to quiet her, and Heidi gave in each time because of a secret delight she had in the thought that every day added two more white rolls to the number she was collecting for grandmother.

After dinner Heidi had to sit alone in her room for a couple of hours. So she had plenty of time to picture how everything at home was now turning green, and how the yellow flowers were shining in the sun. At times her longing to be back home was almost more than she could bear. Dete had told her that she could go home whenever she liked, so one day she decided to leave. In haste she tied all the rolls up in her red shawl, put on her straw hat, and went downstairs. But just as she reached the hall door she met Miss Rottenmeier returning from a walk. The housekeeper stared at her in amazement.

"What do you mean by this?" she demanded. "Have I not forbidden you to go running about in the streets? You look like a beggar."

"I was not going to run about, I was going home," said Heidi, frightened.

"What are you talking about! You want to go home?" exclaimed Miss Rottenmeier, her anger arising. "What would Mrs. Sesemann say if he knew! And what is the matter with his house, I should like to know! Have you not been treated better than you deserved? Have you wanted for a thing? Have you ever in your life before had such a house to live in, such a table, or so many to wait upon you? Have you?"

"No," replied Heidi.

"I should think not indeed!" exclaimed the exasperated lady. "You have everything you can possibly want here, and you are an ungrateful little thing."

Then Heidi's feelings got the better of her, and she poured forth her trouble. "Indeed, I only want to go home, for if I stay so long away Snowflake will begin crying again, and grandmother is waiting for me, and Greenfinch will get beaten, because I am not there to give Peter any cheese, and I can never see how the sun says good night to the mountains. If the great bird were to fly over Frankfurt he would croak louder than ever about people huddling all together and teaching each other bad things, and not going to live up on the rocks, where it is so much better."

"Heaven have mercy on us, the child is out of her mind!" cried Miss Rottenmeier, and she turned in terror and went quickly up the steps, running violently against Sebastian in her hurry. "Go and bring that unhappy little creature in at once," she ordered him, putting her hand to her forehead which she had bumped against his.

Sebastian did as he was told, rubbing his own head as he went, for he had received a still harder blow.

Heidi had not moved. She was trembling all over and her eyes were blazing.

"What, got into trouble again?" said Sebastian in a

cheerful voice. When he looked more closely at Heidi, and saw that she did not move, he put his hand kindly on her shoulder and said, trying to comfort her, "There, there, don't take it to heart so much. Keep up your spirits, that is the great thing!" Then seeing that Heidi still did not stir, "We must go; she ordered me to take you in."

Heidi now began mounting the stairs, but with a slow, crawling step, very unlike her usual manner. Sebastian felt quite sad as he watched her, and as he followed her up he kept trying to encourage her. "Don't you give in! Don't let her make you unhappy! You keep up your courage! The kittens are enjoying themselves very much up in their home. Later we will go up and see them, when Miss Rottenmeier is out of the way, shall we?"

Heidi gave a little nod of assent, but in such a joyless manner that it went to Sebastian's heart. He followed her with sympathetic eyes as she crept away to her room.

At supper that evening Miss Rottenmeier did not speak, but she kept watching Heidi as if she expected her at any minute to break out in some extraordinary way. Heidi sat without moving or eating. However, she did not forget to hide her roll in her pocket.

The next day Miss Rottenmeier made up her mind to add to Heidi's clothing with some garments from Clara's wardrobe, so as to give her a decent appear-

ance when Mr. Sesemann returned. Clara was delighted with the idea, so the housekeeper went upstairs to overhaul Heidi's belongings. She returned,
however, in the course of a few minutes with an expression of horror upon her face.

"What is this, Adelheid, that I find in your wardrobe!" she exclaimed. "A heap of rolls! Will you
believe it, Clara, bread in a wardrobe!" She called
to Tinette to go up and throw away the rolls and the
old straw hat.

"No, no," screamed Heidi. "I must keep the hat,
and the rolls are for grandmother," and she was rushing to stop Tinette when Miss Rottenmeier took hold
of her. "You shall stay right here, and all that bread
and rubbish shall be taken away," she said in a determined tone.

Then Heidi in despair flung herself down on Clara's
chair and broke into a wild fit of weeping. She kept
sobbing out at intervals: "Now grandmother's bread
is all gone! They were all for grandmother, and now
they are taken away, and grandmother won't have
one."

Clara was distressed and alarmed at the child's crying. "Heidi, Heidi," she said imploringly, "please
do not cry so! Listen to me; don't be so unhappy.
Look now, I promise you that you shall have just as
many rolls, or more, all fresh and new to take to
grandmother when you go home. Yours would have

been hard and stale by then. Come, Heidi, do not
cry any more!"

Heidi could not stop crying for a long time. She
would not have been able to stop when she did if it
had not been for Clara's promise, which comforted
her.

Heidi appeared at supper with her eyes red with
weeping, and when she saw her roll she could not
suppress a sob. Whenever Sebastian could catch her
eye he made all sorts of strange signs, pointing to his
own head and then to hers.

When Heidi was going to get into bed that night
she found her old straw hat lying under the counter-
pane. Sebastian had been trying to tell her that he
had saved it for her. She snatched it up with delight,
and after she had wrapped a handkerchief around it,
she stuck it in a corner of the cupboard as far back
as she could.

Mr. Sesemann Hears of Things ✑
Which Are New to Him

A FEW days after these events there was great commotion and much running up and down stairs in Mr. Sesemann's house. The master had just returned, and Sebastian and Tinette were busy carrying up one package after another from the carriage. Mr. Sesemann always brought back a lot of pretty things for his home. He himself had not waited to do anything before going in to see his daughter. Father and daughter greeted each other with warm affection. Then Mr. Sesemann held out his hand to Heidi, who had stolen away into the corner, and said kindly to her: "And this is our little Swiss girl! Come and shake hands with me! That's right! Now, tell me, are Clara and you good friends, or do you get angry and quarrel, and then cry and make it up, and then start quarreling again on the next occasion?"

"No, Clara is always kind to me," answered Heidi.

"And Heidi," put in Clara quickly, "has not once tried to quarrel."

"That's all right, I am glad to hear it," said her father, as he rose from his chair. "But you must excuse me, Clara, for I want my dinner. I have had nothing to eat all day. Afterward I will show you all the things I have brought home with me."

He found Miss Rottenmeier in the dining room superintending the preparation for his meal, and when he had taken his place she sat down opposite him, looking the picture of bad news. "What am I to expect, Miss Rottenmeier?" he asked. "You greet me with an expression that quite frightens me. What is the matter? Clara seems cheerful enough."

"Mr. Sesemann," began the lady in a solemn voice, "it is a matter which concerns Clara; we have been frightfully imposed upon."

"Indeed, in what way?" asked Mr. Sesemann as he went on calmly drinking his coffee.

"We had decided, as you remember, to get a companion for Clara, and as I knew how anxious you were to have only those who were well-behaved and nicely brought up about her, I thought I would look for a little Swiss girl. I hoped to find one such as I have often read about, who, born as it were of the mountain air, lives and moves without touching the earth."

"Still, I think even a Swiss child would have to touch the earth if she wanted to go anywhere," remarked Mr. Sesemann. "Otherwise she would have been given wings instead of feet."

"Ah, Mr. Sesemann, you know what I mean," exclaimed Miss Rottenmeier. "I have been disgracefully imposed upon.

"If you only knew the kind of people and animals she has brought into the house during your absence! The tutor can tell you more about that."

"Animals? What am I to understand by animals, Miss Rottenmeier?"

"It is past understanding; the whole behavior of the child would be past understanding, if it were not that at times she is evidently not in her right mind."

Mr. Sesemann had attached very little importance to what was told him up till now, but this was more serious. It might be harmful to his own child. He looked very narrowly at the lady opposite to assure himself that the mental weakness was not on her side. At that moment the door opened and the tutor was announced.

"Ah! Here is someone," exclaimed Mr. Sesemann, "who will help to clear up matters for me. Take a seat," he continued, as he held out his hand to the tutor. "You will drink a cup of coffee with me. And now tell me, what is the matter with this child that has come to be a companion to my daughter?"

The tutor began in his usual roundabout way, and after several efforts to get a simple statement from him, Mr. Sesemann gave up in despair.

"Excuse me, my dear sir, do not disturb yourself, but I must—I think my daughter will be wanting me," he said, and quickly left the room and took care not to return. He sat down beside his daughter in the study, and turned to Heidi, who had risen, "Little one, will you bring me a glass of water?" he said.

"Fresh water?" asked Heidi.

"Yes—yes—as fresh as you can get it," he answered. Heidi promptly disappeared.

"And now, my dear little Clara," he said, drawing his chair nearer and taking her hand in his, "try to answer my questions clearly. What kind of animals has your little companion brought into the house, and why does Miss Rottenmeier think that she is not always in her right mind?"

Clara told her father everything about the tortoise and the kittens, and explained to him what Heidi had said the day Miss Rottenmeier had been put in such a fright. Mr. Sesemann laughed heartily at her recital. "So you do not want me to send the child home again?" he asked. "You are not tired of having her here?"

"Oh, no, no," Clara exclaimed. "Please do not send her away. Time has passed much more quickly since Heidi has been here, for something new happens every day. It used to be so dull!"

"That's all right then—and here comes your little friend. Have you brought me some good, fresh water?" he asked as Heidi handed him a glass.

"Yes, fresh from the pump," answered Heidi.

"You did not go yourself to the pump?" said Clara.

"Yes, I did. I had to go a long way. There were such a lot of people at the first pump, that I went farther down the street, but there were just as many at the second pump. I was able to get some water at the one in the next street, and the gentleman with the white hair asked me to give his kind regards to Mr. Sesemann."

"You have had quite a successful expedition," said Mr. Sesemann laughing. "And who was the gentleman?"

"He was passing, and when he saw me he stood still and said, 'As you have a glass will you give me a drink? To whom are you taking the water?' When I said, 'To Mr. Sesemann,' he laughed very much, and then he gave me that message for you, and also said he hoped you would enjoy the water."

"I wonder who it was that sent me such good wishes. Tell me what he was like," said Mr. Sesemann.

"He was kind and laughed, and he had a thick gold chain and a gold thing hanging from it with a large red stone, and a horse's head at the top of his stick."

"It's the doctor," exclaimed Clara and her father at the same moment.

That evening Mr. Sesemann told Miss Rottenmeier that he intended to keep Heidi. He found the child in a perfectly right state of mind, he said, and his daughter liked her as a companion. "I want the child to be treated kindly in every way," he continued, "and I do not want her peculiarities to be looked upon as crimes. If you find her too much for you alone, I can hold out a prospect of help, for I am shortly expecting my mother here on a long visit. As you know, she can get along with anybody."

"Oh, yes, I know," replied Miss Rottenmeier, but there was no tone of relief in her voice as she thought of the coming help.

Mr. Sesemann was home for only a short time. He left for Paris again before two weeks were up. He had just gone when a letter came from his mother announcing her arrival on the following day. Clara was overjoyed, and talked so much about her grandmother that evening, that Heidi, too, began to call her "grandmamma."

Another Grandmother ⟋

THERE was much expectation and preparation about the house on the following evening. Tinette had a new white cap on her head. Sebastian collected all the footstools he could find and placed them in convenient spots. Miss Rottenmeier, very straight and dignified, went about inspecting everything.

When the carriage drove up to the door, Tinette and Sebastian ran down the steps, followed with a slower and more stately step by Miss Rottenmeier. Heidi had been sent up to her room and ordered to remain there until she was called. She had not long to wait before Tinette put her head in and said abruptly, "Go downstairs into the study."

As Heidi opened the study door she heard a kind voice say: "Ah, here comes the child! Come along and let me have a good look at you."

Heidi walked up to her and said very distinctly in her clear voice, "Good evening."

The grandmother patted Heidi's cheeks and smiled at her and the child looked back at her with steady, serious eyes. Everything about the grandmother at-

111

tracted her, so that she could not turn her eyes away. She had such beautiful white hair, and two long lace ends hung down from the cap on her head and waved gently about her face every time she moved, as if a soft breeze were blowing round her. That gave Heidi a peculiar feeling of pleasure.

"And what is your name, child?" the grandmother now asked.

"I am always called 'Heidi'; but as I am now to be called 'Adelheid,' I will try to take care—"

"Mrs. Sesemann will no doubt agree with me," Miss Rottenmeier interrupted, "that it was necessary to choose a name that could be pronounced easily, if only for the sake of the servants."

"My good Rottenmeier," replied Mrs. Sesemann, "if a person is called 'Heidi' and has grown accustomed to that name, I call her 'Heidi.'"

Miss Rottenmeier was always very much annoyed that the old lady continually addressed her by her surname only; but it did no good to object for the grandmother always went her own way.

The next afternoon while Clara was resting, the grandmother went up to Miss Rottenmeier's room and gave a loud knock at the door. Miss Rottenmeier opened the door and drew back in surprise at this unexpected visit.

"Where is the child, and what is she doing all this time?" asked Mrs. Sesemann.

"She is sitting in her room, where she could well employ herself if she had the least idea of making herself useful; but you have no idea, Mrs. Sesemann, of the out-of-the-way things this child imagines and does, things which I could hardly repeat in good society."

"I should do the same if I had to sit in there like that child, I can tell you. Go and get the child and bring her to my room. I have some pretty books with me that I should like to give her."

"That is just the misfortune," said Miss Rottenmeier with a despairing gesture. "What use are books to her? She has not been able to learn even her A B C's, all the long time she has been here. If the tutor had not the patience of an angel he would have given up teaching her long ago."

"That is very strange," said Mrs. Sesemann. "She does not look to me like a child who would be unable to learn her alphabet. However, bring her to me now. She can at least amuse herself with the pictures in the books."

Heidi soon appeared. She gazed with open-eyed delight and wonder at the beautiful, colored pictures in the books which the grandmother gave her to look at. All of a sudden, as she turned a page to a fresh picture, the child gave a cry. For a moment or two she looked at it with brightening eyes, then the tears began to fall, and at last she burst into sobs. The grandmother looked at the picture. It represented a green pasture, full of young animals, some grazing and others nibbling at the shrubs. In the middle was a shepherd leaning upon his staff and looking on at his happy flock. The whole scene was bathed in golden light, for the sun was just sinking below the horizon.

The grandmother laid her hand kindly on Heidi's. "Don't cry, dear child, don't cry," she said. "The picture has perhaps reminded you of something. But see, there is a beautiful story to the picture which I will tell you this evening. And there are other stories of all kinds to read and to tell again. But now we must have a little talk together, so dry your tears and come and stand in front of me, so that I may see you well. There, now we are happy again."

But it was some little time before Heidi could overcome her sobs. The grandmother gave her time to recover herself, saying cheering words to her now and then, "There, it's all right now, and we are quite happy again."

When at last she saw that Heidi was growing calmer, she said: "Now I want you to tell me something. How are you getting on in your schoolwork? Do you like your lessons, and have you learned a great deal?"

"Oh, no!" replied Heidi, sighing. "But I knew beforehand that it was not possible to learn."

"What is it you think impossible to learn?"

"Why, to read. It is too hard."

"You don't say so! And who told you that?"

"Peter told me, and he knew all about it, for he had tried and tried and could not learn it."

"Peter must be a very odd boy then! But listen, Heidi, we must not always go by what Peter says, we must try for ourselves. I am certain that you did not give all your attention to the tutor when he was trying to teach you your letters."

"It's of no use," said Heidi in the tone of one who was ready to endure what could not be cured.

"Listen to what I have to say," commanded the grandmother. "You have not been able to learn your alphabet because you believed what Peter said. Now you must believe what I tell you, and I tell you that you can learn to read in a very little while, as many children do, who are made like you and not like Peter. You see that picture with the shepherd and the animals? Well, as soon as you are able to read you shall have that book for your own, and then you will know all about the sheep and the goats, and what the shepherd did, and the wonderful things that happened to him. You will like that, won't you?"

Heidi had listened with eager attention to the grandmother's words and now with a sigh exclaimed, "Oh, if only I could read now!"

"It won't take you long now to learn, I can see. Now we must go down to Clara. Bring the books with you." And hand in hand the two went over to the study.

Since the day when Heidi had tried to go home, a change had come over her. She had at last understood that she could not go home when she wished as Dete had told her, but that she would have to stay on in Frankfurt for a long, long time, perhaps forever. She had also understood that Mr. Sesemann would think it ungrateful of her if she wished to leave, and she believed that the grandmother and Clara would think the same.

But the weight of trouble on the little heart grew heavier and heavier. She could no longer eat her food, and every day she grew a little paler. She lay awake for long hours at night, for as soon as she was alone and everything was still around her, the picture of the mountain with its sunshine and flowers rose vividly before her eyes. When at last she fell asleep it was to dream of the rocks and the snowfield turning crimson in the evening light. When she awoke in the morning she would think herself back at the hut and prepare to run joyfully out into the sun—and then— here was her large bed, and here she was in Frankfurt far, far away from home. And Heidi would often weep for a long time, with her face buried in the pillow so that no one would hear her.

Heidi's unhappiness did not escape the grandmother's notice. She let some days go by to see if

the child grew brighter and lost her downcast appearance. But as matters did not mend, and she saw that
many mornings Heidi had evidently been crying before she came downstairs, she took her again into her
room one day, and drawing the child to her, said,
"Now tell me, Heidi, what is the matter? Are you
in trouble?"

But Heidi was afraid if she told the truth that the
grandmother would think her ungrateful, and would
stop being so kind to her, so she answered, "I can't
tell you."

"Well, could you tell Clara about it?"

"Oh, no, I cannot tell anyone," said Heidi in so
positive a tone, and with a look of such trouble on
her face, that the grandmother felt full of pity for the
child.

"Then, dear child, let me tell you what to do. You
know that when we are in great trouble, and cannot
speak about it to anybody, we must turn to God and
pray Him to help, for He can deliver us from everything that worries us. You understand that, do you
not? You say your prayers every evening to God in
Heaven, and thank Him for all He has done for you,
and pray Him to keep you from all evil, do you not?"

"No, I never say any prayers," answered Heidi.

"Have you never been taught to pray, Heidi? Do
you not even know what it means?"

"I used to say prayers with the first grandmother,

but that is a long time ago, and I have forgotten them."

"That is the reason, Heidi, that you are so unhappy, because you know no one who can help you. Think what a comfort it is when we feel sad to be able at any moment to go and tell everything to God. He can help us and give us everything that will make us happy again."

A sudden gleam of joy came into Heidi's eyes. "May I tell Him everything, everything?"

"Yes, everything, Heidi, everything."

Heidi drew her hand away, which the grandmother was holding affectionately between her own, and said quickly, "May I go?"

"Yes, of course," was the answer, and Heidi ran out of the room and into her own. Sitting down on a stool, she folded her hands together and told God about everything that was making her so sad and unhappy, and begged Him earnestly to help her and to let her go home to her grandfather.

It was about a week after this that the tutor asked Mrs. Sesemann's permission for an interview with her. He told her that Heidi had at last learned to read, and, unlike most beginners, had read correctly from the first.

Mrs. Sesemann was delighted. When the tutor had gone, she went down to the study to make sure of the good news. Heidi was sitting beside Clara, reading aloud to her. She was growing more and more delighted with the new world that was open to her as the black letters grew alive and turned into men and things and exciting stories. That same evening Heidi found the large book with the beautiful pictures lying on her plate when she took her place at the table. When she looked questioningly at the grandmother, Mrs. Sesemann nodded kindly to her and said, "Yes, it's yours now."

"Mine, to keep always? Even when I go home?" said Heidi, blushing with pleasure.

"Yes, of course, yours forever," she assured her. "Tomorrow we will begin to read it."

"But you are not going home yet, Heidi, not for years," put in Clara. "When grandmother goes away, I shall want you to stay on with me."

When Heidi went to her room that night she had another look at her book before she went to bed. From that day forth her chief pleasure was to read the tales which belonged to the beautiful pictures over and over again. If the grandmother said, as they were sitting together in the evening, "Now Heidi will read aloud to us," Heidi was delighted, for reading was no trouble to her now. When she read the tales aloud the scenes seemed to grow more beautiful and distinct.

Heidi Gains in One Way 🖎
and Loses in Another

Every afternoon, while Clara was resting, the grandmother took Heidi into her room. She had a lot of pretty dolls, and she showed Heidi how to make dresses for them. Then grandmother liked to hear Heidi read aloud, and the oftener she read her tales, the fonder she grew of them. Still Heidi never looked really happy, and her eyes were no longer bright. In the last week of the grandmother's visit, she called Heidi into her room as usual one day after dinner. The child came with her book under her arm. The grandmother called her to come close, and then laying the book aside, said, "Now, child, tell me why you are not happy. Have you still the same trouble at heart?"

Heidi nodded in reply.

"Have you told God about it?"

"Yes."

"And do you pray every day that He will make things right and that you may be happy again?"

"No, I have stopped praying."

"Do not tell me that, Heidi! Why have you stopped praying?"

"It is of no use, God does not listen," Heidi said in a trembling voice. "I can understand that when there are so many, many people in Frankfurt praying to Him every evening He cannot answer all the prayers. He certainly has not heard what I said to Him."

"And why are you so sure of that, Heidi?"

"Because I have prayed for the same thing every day for a long time, and yet God has not done what I asked."

"You are wrong, Heidi. You must not think of Him like that. God is a good Father to us all, and knows better than we do what is good for us. If we ask Him for something that is not good for us, He does not give it, but He does give something better still, if only we will continue to pray earnestly and do not run away and lose our trust in Him. God did not think what you have been praying for was good for you just now; but be sure He heard you, for He can hear and see everyone at the same time, because He is God and not a human being like you and me. And because He thought it was better for you not to have at once what you wanted, He said to Himself: 'Yes, Heidi shall have what she asks for, but not until the right time comes, so that she may be quite happy.

If I do what she wants now, and then one day she sees that it would have been better for her not to have had her own way, she will cry and say, "If only God had not given me what I asked for! It is not so good as I expected!" ' And while God is watching over you, and looking to see if you will trust Him and go on praying to Him every day, and turn to Him for everything you want, you run away and stop saying your prayers, and forget all about Him. You would not like to grieve God, would you, Heidi, when He wants only to be kind to you? So will you not go and ask Him to forgive you, and continue to pray and to trust Him? You may be sure that He will make everything right and happy for you, and then you will be glad and lighthearted again."

Heidi had perfect confidence in the grandmother, and every word she said sank into her heart.

"I will go at once and ask God to forgive me, and I will never forget Him again," she replied repentantly.

"That is right, dear child." Anxious to cheer her, the grandmother added, "Don't be unhappy, for He will do everything you wish in good time."

Heidi ran away and prayed that she might always remember God, and that He would go on thinking about her.

The day came for grandmother's departure—a sad day for Clara and Heidi. But the grandmother was determined to make it as much like a holiday as possible and not to let them mope, and she kept them so lively and amused that they had no time to think about their sorrow at her going until she really drove away. Then the house seemed so silent and empty that Heidi and Clara did not know what to do with themselves, and sat during the remainder of the day like two lost children.

The next day, when the hour came for the children to be together, Heidi walked in with her book and proposed that she should go on reading aloud every afternoon to Clara. Clara agreed, so Heidi began with her usual enthusiasm. But the reading did not last long, for Heidi had hardly begun a tale about a dying grandmother before she cried out, "Oh! then grandmother is dead!" and burst into tears. Everything she read was so real to her that she quite thought it was the grandmother at home who had died, and she kept on exclaiming as her sobs increased, "She is dead, and I shall never see her again, and she never had one of the white rolls!"

Clara did all she could to explain to Heidi that the story was about quite a different grandmother. Even when at last she had been able to convince Heidi of this, the little girl continued to weep inconsolably, for now she had awakened to the thought that perhaps the grandmother, and even the grandfather also, might die while she was so far away. She thought if she did not go home for a long time she would find everything there all silent and dead. She would be all alone, and would never be able to see the dear ones she loved any more.

Miss Rottenmeier had meanwhile come into the room, and Clara explained to her what had happened. As Heidi continued her weeping, the lady, who was evidently getting impatient with her, went up to her and said with decision, "Now, Adelheid, that is enough of all this causeless lamentation. I tell you once for all, if there are any more scenes like this while you are reading, I shall take the book away from you and shall not let you have it again."

Her words had immediate effect on Heidi, who turned pale with fear. The book was her one great treasure. She quickly dried her tears and swallowed her sobs as best she could, so that no further sound of them should be heard. The threat did its work, for Heidi never cried aloud again whatever she might be reading, but she had often to struggle hard to keep back her tears, so that Clara would look at her and say, "What faces you are making, Heidi, I never saw anything like it!" But the faces made no noise and did not offend Miss Rottenmeier.

Heidi lost all her appetite, and looked so pale and thin that Sebastian was quite unhappy when he looked at her, and could not bear to see her refusing all the good dishes he handed her. She hardly ate anything at all, and as soon as she laid her head down at night the picture of home would rise before her eyes, and she would weep, burying her face in the pillow so that her crying might not be heard.

And so many weeks passed away. Heidi's longing for the old, familiar, beautiful things grew daily stronger, so that now only to read a word that recalled them to her brought her to the verge of tears, which she kept back with difficulty. So the autumn and winter passed, and again the sun came shining down on the white walls of the opposite houses. Heidi would think to herself that now the time had come for Peter to go out again with the goats to where the golden rockroses were glowing in the sunlight and all the rocks around turned to fire at sunset. She would go and sit in a corner of her lonely room and put her hands over her eyes that she might not see the sun shining on the opposite wall. There she would remain without moving, battling silently with her terrible homesickness, until Clara sent for her again.

A Ghost in the House ⌒

For some days past Miss Rottenmeier had gone
about rather silently, as if lost in thought. As
twilight fell, and she passed from room to room, or
through the long corridors, she looked cautiously behind her, as if she thought someone was coming up
silently behind her. If she visited the upper floor
where the grand guest chambers were, or had to go
down into the large, mysterious council chamber,
where every footstep echoed, she regularly called
Tinette to accompany her, in case, as she said, there
might be something to carry up or down. Tinette
on her side did exactly the same. If she had business
upstairs or down, she called Sebastian to accompany
her. More curious still, Sebastian also, if sent into
one of the more distant rooms, always called John,
the coachman, to go with him. John readily obeyed,
for he did not know how soon he might want to ask
Sebastian to do the same service for him. And while
these things were going on upstairs, the cook, who
had been in the house for years, would shake her head

over her pots and kettles and sigh, "That ever I should
live to know such a thing!"

For something very strange and mysterious was going on in Mr. Sesemann's house. Every morning,
when the servants went downstairs, they found the
front door wide open. The first morning they
thought the house must have been robbed, but nothing was missing. The door was doubly locked at
night, and for further security the wooden bar was
fastened across it, but all this did no good.

At last, Sebastian and John plucked up courage
and agreed to sit up one night to watch. At first they
talked, but soon they grew drowsy and at last fell
asleep. When one o'clock struck they roused themselves and with a great show of courage went out into
the hall.

Just as they did so, a sudden gust of air blew through
the open front door and put out the light which John
held in his hand. He started back, almost overturning
Sebastian. Without speaking, he clutched the surprised Sebastian and pulled him back into the room.
Shutting the door quickly he turned the key as far as
he could make it go. Then he pulled out his matches
and lighted his candle again. Sebastian, in the sudden-
ness of the affair, did not know exactly what had
happened, for he had not seen the open door nor felt
the breeze. But now, as he saw the coachman in the
light, he gave a cry of alarm, for John was trembling

all over and was as white as a ghost. "What's the matter? What did you see outside?" asked Sebastian sympathetically.

"The door partly open," gasped John, "and a white figure standing at the top of the steps. There it stood, and then all in a minute it disappeared."

Sebastian felt his blood run cold. The two sat down close to one another and did not dare move again till the morning broke and the streets began to be alive again. Then they left the room together, shut the front door, and went upstairs to tell Miss Rottenmeier of their experience. She was quite ready to receive them, for she had not been able to sleep at all in her anxiety to hear their report. As soon as they had given her details of the night's experience she sat down and wrote to Mr. Sesemann. She could hardly write, she told him, for her fingers were stiff with fear. He must please arrange to come back at once, for dreadful and unaccountable things were taking place at home. Then she entered into particulars of all that had happened.

Mr. Sesemann answered that it was quite impossible for him to arrange to leave his business. He told Miss Rottenmeier to write to his mother and ask her to come. He was sure she would soon find a way to deal with the ghost. Miss Rottenmeier was not pleased with the tone of this letter; she did not think the matter was treated seriously enough. She wrote off without delay to Mrs. Sesemann, but got no more satisfactory reply from that quarter.

As soon as the housekeeper had received Mrs. Sesemann's letter she walked straight into the study, and there in a low, mysterious voice told the two children everything that had taken place. Clara immediately screamed out that she could not remain another minute alone, her father must come home, and Miss Rottenmeier must sleep in her room at night, and Heidi too must not be left by herself, for the ghost might do something. Heidi, however, was unmoved by the story, for she had never heard of ghosts before.

As soon as Miss Rottenmeier had succeeded in quieting Clara, she sat down to write another letter to Mr. Sesemann. She told him that these unaccountable things that were going on in the house had so affected his daughter's delicate constitution that the worst consequences might be expected.

The letter was successful, and two days later Mr. Sesemann reached home. He went up without a moment's delay into his daughter's room. Clara greeted him with a cry of joy. When he saw her so lively and apparently as well as ever, his face cleared.

"And how is the ghost getting on?" he asked, turning to Miss Rottenmeier, with a twinkle of amusement in his eye.

"It is no joke, I assure you," replied that lady. "You will not laugh yourself tomorrow morning, Mr.

Sesemann. What is going on in the house points to some terrible thing that has taken place in the past and been concealed."

"Well, I know nothing about that," said the master of the house, "but I must beg you not to bring suspicion on my worthy ancestors. And now will you kindly call Sebastian into the dining room. I wish to speak to him alone."

"Come here, lad," he said as Sebastian appeared, "Have you been playing at ghosts to amuse yourself at Miss Rottenmeier's expense?"

"No, on my honor, sir. Pray, do not think it. I am very uncomfortable about the matter myself," answered Sebastian with unmistakable truthfulness.

"Well, if that is so, I will show you and John tomorrow morning how ghosts look in the daylight. You ought to be ashamed of yourself, Sebastian, a great strong lad like you, to run away from a ghost! But now take a message to my friend the doctor. Ask if he will come to me tonight at nine o'clock without fail. Tell him I have come by express from Paris to consult him. It is such a bad case I shall want him to spend the night here. You understand?"

"Yes, sir," replied Sebastian, "I will see to the matter as you wish."

Mr. Sesemann returned to Clara, and begged her to have no more fear, for he would soon find out all about the ghost and put an end to it.

Punctually at nine o'clock the doctor arrived. He was a gray-haired man with a fresh face, and bright, kindly eyes. He looked anxious as he walked in, but, on catching sight of his patient burst out laughing and clapped him on the shoulder.

"Well," he said, "you look pretty bad for a person that I am to sit up with all night."

"Patience, friend," answered Mr. Sesemann. "The one you have to sit up for will look a good deal worse when we have once caught him."

"So there is a sick person in the house, and one that has first to be caught?"

"Much worse than that, doctor; a ghost in the house! My house is haunted!"

The doctor laughed aloud.

"That's a nice way of showing sympathy, doctor!" exclaimed Mr. Sesemann. "It's a pity my friend Rottenmeier cannot hear you. She is firmly convinced that some old member of the family is wandering about the house doing penance for some awful crime."

"How did she become acquainted with him?" asked the doctor, still very much amused.

Mr. Sesemann told him the story of the open front door.

The two took up their quarters for the night in the same room in which Sebastian and John had kept watch. Two loaded revolvers lay on the table. Two good-sized lamps had also been lighted, for Mr. Sesemann was determined not to wait for ghosts in any half-light.

The door was shut close to prevent the lights shining into the hall outside and frightening away the ghost. The two gentlemen sat comfortably back in the armchairs and began talking of all sorts of things. So twelve o'clock struck before they were aware.

"The ghost has got scent of us and is keeping away tonight," said the doctor.

"Wait a bit, it does not generally appear before one o'clock," answered his friend.

They started talking again. One o'clock struck. There was not a sound about the house, nor in the street outside. Suddenly the doctor lifted his finger.

"Hush! Sesemann, don't you hear something?"

They both listened, and they distinctly heard the bar on the front door softly pushed aside and then the key turned in the lock and the door opened. Mr. Sesemann put out his hand for his revolver.

"You are not afraid, are you?" said the doctor as he stood up.

"It is better to take precautions," whispered Mr. Sesemann, and seizing one of the lights in his other hand, he followed the doctor, who, likewise armed with a light and a revolver, went quietly on ahead. They stepped into the hall. The moonlight was shining in through the open door and fell on a white figure standing motionless in the doorway.

"Who is there?" thundered the doctor in a voice that echoed through the hall, as the two men advanced toward the figure.

It turned and gave a low cry. There in her little white nightgown stood Heidi, staring with wild eyes at the lights and the revolvers, and trembling from head to foot like a leaf in the wind. The two men looked at one another in surprise.

"Why, I believe it is your little water carrier, Sesemann," said the doctor.

"Child, what does this mean?" said Mr. Sesemann. "What did you want? Why did you come down here?"

White with terror, and hardly able to make her voice heard, Heidi answered, "I don't know."

But now the doctor stepped forward. "This is a matter for me to see to, Sesemann. Go back to your chair. I must take the child upstairs to her bed."

And with that he put down his revolver and gently taking the child by the hand led her upstairs. "Don't be frightened," he said as they went up side by side. "It's nothing to be frightened about. It's all right, only just go quietly."

When they reached Heidi's room the doctor put the little girl in bed and covered her up carefully. Sitting down beside her he waited until she had grown quieter and no longer trembled so violently. Then he took her hand and said in a kind, soothing voice,

"There, now you feel better. Tell me where you wanted to go."

"I did not want to go anywhere," said Heidi. "I did not know I went downstairs, but all at once I was there."

"I see, and had you been dreaming, so that you seemed to see and hear something very distinctly?"

"Yes, I dream every night, and always about the same things. I think I am back with grandfather, and I hear the sound in the fir trees outside, and I see the stars shining so brightly, and then I open the door quickly and run out, and it is all so beautiful! But when I wake I am still in Frankfurt." And Heidi struggled as she spoke to keep back the sobs which seemed to choke her.

"And have you no pain anywhere? No pain in your head or back?"

"No, only a feeling as if there were a great stone weighing on me."

"As if you had eaten something that would not go down."

"No, not like that; something heavy, as if I wanted to cry hard."

"I see, and then do you have a good cry?"

"Oh, no, I mustn't. Miss Rottenmeier forbade me to cry."

"So you swallow it all down, I suppose? Are you happy here in Frankfurt?"

"Yes," was the low answer, but it sounded more like "No."

"And where did you live with your grandfather?"

"Up on the mountain."

"That wasn't very amusing; rather dull at times, eh?"

"No, no, it was beautiful, beautiful!" Heidi could go no further. The remembrance of the past, the excitement she had just gone through, the long-suppressed weeping, were too much for the child's strength. The tears began to fall fast, and she broke into violent weeping.

The doctor stood up. "There, there, go on crying," he said kindly. "It will do you good. Then go to sleep. It will be all right tomorrow."

He went downstairs to his friend. "Sesemann," he said, "let me first tell you that your little charge is a sleepwalker. She is the ghost who has nightly opened the front door and put your household into this fever of alarm. Secondly, the child is consumed with homesickness, to such an extent that she is nearly a skeleton already, and soon will be quite one. Something must be done at once. For the first trouble, due to her overexcited nerves, there is but one remedy, to send her back to her native mountain air. For the second trouble there is also but one cure, and that is the same. So tomorrow the child must start for home. There you have my prescription."

Mr. Sesemann had risen and now paced up and down the room in concern.

"What!" he exclaimed. "The child a sleepwalker and ill! Homesick, and grown emaciated in my house! All this has taken place in my house and no one has seen or known anything about it. And you mean, doctor, that the child who came here happy and healthy I am to send back to her grandfather a miserable little skeleton? I can't do it; you cannot dream of my doing such a thing! Take the child in hand, do with her what you will, and make her whole and sound, and then she shall go home; but you must do something first."

"Sesemann," replied the doctor, "consider what you are doing! This illness of the child's is not one to be cured with pills and powders. She has not a tough constitution, but if you send her back at once she may recover in the mountain air, if not—you would rather she went back ill than not at all?"

Mr. Sesemann stood still; the doctor's words were a shock to him.

"If you put it so, doctor, there is assuredly only one way—and the thing must be seen to at once." They walked up and down for a while arranging what to do; then the doctor left.

A Summer Evening ✑
On the Mountain

MR. SESEMANN, a good deal annoyed and excited, went quickly upstairs and knocked on Miss Rottenmeier's door. "Please make haste and come down to me in the dining room!" he called. "We must make ready for a journey at once." Miss Rottenmeier looked at her clock: it was just four-thirty. She had never risen so early before in her life. What could have happened? She was so filled with curiosity and excitement that she took hold of everything the wrong way. In her haste she kept on searching everywhere for garments which she had already put on.

Meanwhile Mr. Sesemann had rung the bells in turn which communicated with the several servants' rooms, causing frightened figures to leap out of bed, convinced that the ghost had attacked the master and that he was calling for help. One by one they made their appearance in the dining room, each with a more terrified face than the last, and were astonished to see their master walking up and down, looking perfectly well, and with no appearance of having had an encounter with a ghost. John was sent off without delay to get the horses and carriage ready; Tinette was ordered to wake Heidi and get her dressed for a journey; Sebastian was hurried off to the house where Dete was in service to bring her around. Miss Rottenmeier was directed to pack a trunk at once for Heidi. She was disappointed, for she had hoped to have the mystery explained. But Mr. Sesemann had no thought or time for explanations and left her standing there while he went to speak to Clara.

He sat down beside his little daughter and told her everything that had occurred during the past night. He repeated the doctor's verdict and told Clara that he had decided to send Heidi home at once.

Clara was very much distressed, and at first made all kinds of suggestions for keeping Heidi with her. Her father was firm, however, and promised her, if she would be reasonable and make no further fuss, that he would take her to Switzerland next summer. So Clara made no further objection. She insisted that Heidi's trunk be brought into her room to be packed, so that she might add whatever she liked, and her father was only too pleased to let her provide a good outfit for the child.

Meanwhile Dete had arrived. When Mr. Sesemann asked her to take Heidi home she at once began to make excuses. Mr. Sesemann dismissed her and sent for Sebastian. He told the butler he was to travel with the child as far as Basle that day, and the next day take her home. He would give him a letter to the grandfather, which would explain everything.

"But there is one thing in particular which I wish you to look after," said Mr. Sesemann in conclusion, "and be sure you listen well to what I say. I know the people of the hotel in Basle where I want you to go. When you get there, go at once into the child's room and see that the windows are all firmly fastened so that they cannot be easily opened. After she is in bed, lock the door of her room on the outside, for she walks in her sleep and might run into danger in a strange house if she went wandering downstairs and tried to open the front door."

"Oh! Then that was it?" exclaimed Sebastian, for now a light was thrown on the ghostly visitations.

"Yes, that was it! You are a coward, and you may tell John he is the same, and the whole household a pack of idiots." And with this, Mr. Sesemann went off to his study to write a letter to Alm-Uncle.

When the letter was finished, Mr. Sesemann went into the dining room. Breakfast was now ready, and he asked, "Where is the child?"

Heidi was brought in, and as she walked up to him to say, "Good morning," he looked inquiringly into her face and said, "Well, what do you say to this, little one?"

Heidi looked at him in perplexity.

"Why, you don't know anything about it, I see," laughed Mr. Sesemann. "You are going home today, going at once."

"Home?" murmured Heidi in a low voice, turning pale. She was so overcome that for a moment or two she could hardly breathe.

"Don't you want to hear more about it?"

"Oh, yes, yes!" exclaimed Heidi, her face now rosy with delight.

"All right, then," said Mr. Sesemann as he sat down and motioned her to take her place. "Eat a good breakfast, and then off you go in the carriage."

But Heidi could not swallow a morsel though she tried to. She was in such a state of excitement that she hardly knew whether she was awake or dreaming.

"Run up to Clara and stay with her till the carriage comes around," Mr. Sesemann said kindly.

Heidi had been longing for this, and ran quickly upstairs. An immense trunk was standing open in the middle of the room.

"Come along, Heidi," cried Clara, as she entered. "See all the things I have had put in for you. Aren't you pleased?"

And she ran over a list of things, dresses and aprons and handerchiefs, and all kinds of working materials.

"And look here," she added, as she triumphantly held up a basket. Heidi peeped in and jumped for joy, for inside it were twelve beautiful, round, white rolls, all for grandmother. In their delight the children forgot that the time had come for them to separate, and when someone called out, "The carriage is here," there was no time for grieving.

Heidi ran to her room to get her darling book. This was put in the basket with the rolls. Then she opened her wardrobe to look for another treasure, which no one would have thought of packing—the old red scarf. Heidi wrapped it around something else which she laid on the top of the basket, so that the red package was quite conspicuous. Then she put on her pretty hat and left the room.

The children could not spend much time over their farewells, for Mr. Sesemann was waiting to put Heidi in the carriage. Miss Rottenmeier stood at the top of the stairs to say good-by to her. When she caught sight of the strange little red bundle, she took it out of the basket and threw it on the ground.

"No, no, Adelheid," she exclaimed, "you cannot leave the house with that thing. What can you possibly want with it!" And then she said good-by to the child.

Heidi did not dare take up her little bundle, but she gave the master of the house an imploring look, as if her greatest treasure had been taken from her.

"No, no," said Mr. Sesemann in a very decided voice, "the child shall take home with her whatever she likes, kittens and tortoises, if it pleases her. We need not put ourselves out about that, Miss Rotten-meier."

Heidi quickly picked up her bundle, with a look of joy and gratitude. As she stood by the carriage door, Mr. Sesemann gave her his hand and said he hoped she would remember him and Clara. He wished her a happy journey, and Heidi thanked him for all his kindness, and added, "And please say good-by to the doctor for me and give him many, many thanks." She had not forgotten that he had said to her the night before, "It will be all right tomorrow," and she rightly guessed that he had helped to make it so for her. Heidi was now lifted into the carriage, and then the basket and the provisions were put in, and finally Sebastian took his place. Then Mr. Sese-mann called out once more, "A pleasant journey to you," and the carriage rolled away.

Heidi was soon sitting in the railway carriage, hold-ing her basket carefully on her lap. She would not let it out of her hands for a moment, for it contained the delicious rolls for grandmother. For many hours she sat as still as a mouse. She was just beginning to realize that she was going home to grandfather, the mountain, the grandmother, and Peter. Pictures of all she was going to see again rose one by one before her eyes. Her only fear was that the grandmother was dead.

After a while Heidi fell asleep, and after her disturbed night and early rising she slept so soundly that she did not wake till Sebastian shook her by the arm and called to her, "Wake up, wake up! We shall have to get out in a minute. We are just in Basle!"

There was a further railway journey of many hours the next day. All of a sudden, before Heidi expected it, a voice called out, "Mayenfeld." In another minute they were standing on the platform with Heidi's trunk beside them, and the train was steaming away down the valley. Sebastian looked after it regretfully, for he preferred the easier mode of traveling to a wearisome climb on foot, especially as there was no doubt danger as well as fatigue in a country like this.

Just outside the station he saw a shabby-looking little cart which a broad-shouldered man was loading with heavy sacks. Sebastian went up to him and asked how a trunk could be taken up to Dörfli. It was finally agreed that the man should take both the child and the trunk to Dörfli, and there find someone who could be sent on with Heidi up the mountain.

"I can go by myself, I know the way well from Dörfli," put in Heidi, who had been listening attentively to the conversation. Sebastian was greatly relieved at not having to do any mountain climbing.

He drew Heidi aside and gave her a thick package
and a letter for her grandfather. The package, he
told her, contained money for her from Mr. Sesemann, and she must put it at the bottom of her basket
under the rolls and be very careful not to loose it.

Heidi at once put the package and the letter at the
bottom of her basket. The trunk, meanwhile, had
been hoisted into the cart, and now Sebastian lifted
Heidi and her basket up on the high seat and shook
hands with her. The driver swung himself up beside
Heidi, and the cart rolled away in the direction of
the mountains, while Sebastian sat down in the station
to await the return train.

The driver of the cart was the miller at Dörfli and
was taking home his sacks of flour. He had never
seen Heidi, but, like everybody in Dörfli, he knew all
about her. He felt sure at once that this was the
child of whom he had heard so much. He began to
wonder why she had come back, and entered into
conversation with her. "You are the child who
lived with your grandfather, Alm-Uncle, are you
not?"

"Yes."

"Didn't they treat you well down there, that you
have come back so soon?"

"Yes, it was not that. Everything in Frankfurt is as
nice as it could be."

"Then why are you running home again?"

"Only because Mr. Sesemann gave me leave, or else I should not have come."

"If they were willing to let you stay, why did you not remain where you were better off than at home?"

"Because I would a thousand times rather be with grandfather on the mountain than anywhere else in the world."

"You will think differently perhaps when you get back there," grumbled the miller; and then to himself, "It's strange of her, for she must know what it's like."

He began whistling and said no more, and Heidi looked around her. She was beginning to tremble with excitement. She felt as if she must jump down from the cart and run with all her might till she reached the top. The clock was striking five as they drove into Dörfli. A crowd of women and children immediately surrounded the cart, for the arrival of the child and her trunk excited the curiosity of everybody in the neighborhood. As the miller lifted Heidi down, she said hastily, "Thank you, grandfather will send for the trunk." She was going to run off, when first one and then another of the bystanders caught hold of her, each one having a different question to put to her. But Heidi pushed her way through them with such an expression of distress on her face that they were forced to let her go.

Heidi climbed up the steep path from Dörfli as quickly as she could. She was obliged, however, to

pause now and again to take breath, for the basket she
carried was rather heavy, and the way got steeper
as she drew nearer the top. One thought alone filled
Heidi's mind. Would she find the grandmother sitting in her usual corner by the spinning wheel? Was
she still alive? At last Heidi caught sight of the grandmother's house in the hollow of the mountain and her
heart began to beat more quickly. She ran faster and
faster and her heart beat louder and louder. Then she
had reached the house, but she trembled so she could
hardly open the door. Then she was standing inside,
unable in her breathlessness to utter a sound.

"Ah, my God!" cried a voice from the corner.
"that was how Heidi used to run in. If only I could
have her with me once again! Who is there?"

"It's I, I, Grandmother," cried Heidi as she ran
and flung herself on her knees beside the old woman,
and seizing her hands, clung to her, unable to speak
for joy. And the grandmother herself could not say
a word for some time, so unexpected was this happiness. But at last she put out her hand and stroked
Heidi's curly hair, and said, "Yes, yes, that is her hair,
and her voice. Thank God He has granted my
prayer!" And tears of joy fell from the blind eyes
upon Heidi's hand. "Is it really you, Heidi? Have
you really come back to me?"

"Yes, grandmother, I am really here," answered
Heidi in a reassuring voice. "Do not cry, for I have

really come back and I am never going away again, and I shall come every day to see you. You won't have any more hard bread to eat for a while, for look, look!"

And Heidi took the rolls from the basket, and piled the whole twelve up on grandmother's lap.

"Ah, child! Child! What a blessing you bring with you!" the old woman exclaimed, as she felt and seemed never to come to the end of the rolls. "But you yourself are the greatest blessing, Heidi," and again she touched the child's hair and passed her hand over her hot cheeks. "Say something, child, that I may hear your voice," she begged.

While Heidi was talking Peter's mother came in and stood for a moment overcome with astonishment. "Why, it's Heidi!" she exclaimed, "and yet can it be?"

Heidi stood up, and Brigitta could not say enough in admiration of the child's dress and appearance.

"You may have my hat if you like," said Heidi. "I do not want it, I have my own still." She opened her red bundle and took out her own old hat, which had become a little more battered during the journey. She had not forgotten how her grandfather had called out to Dete that he never wished to see her and her hat and feathers again. That was why she had so anxiously kept her old hat, for she had never ceased to think about going home to her grandfather. Brigitta would not take the beautiful new hat, but Heidi quietly hid it in a corner behind the grandmother's chair. Then she took off her pretty dress and put her red shawl on over her petticoat.

"I must go home to grandfather," she said, "but tomorrow I shall come again. Good night, grandmother."

"Yes, come again, be sure you come again tomorrow," begged the grandmother, as she pressed Heidi's hands in hers, unwilling to let her go.

"Why have you taken off that pretty dress?" asked Brigitta.

"Because I would rather go home to grandfather as I am, or else perhaps he would not know me. You hardly did at first."

Heidi bade Brigitta good night and continued her way up the mountain. All around her the steep green slopes shone bright in the evening sun, and soon the great, gleaming snow field up above came in sight. Heidi kept pausing to look around, for the higher peaks were behind her as she climbed. Suddenly a warm red glow fell on the grass at her feet. She looked back again; she had not remembered how splendid it was, nor seen anything to compare to it in her dreams. There the two high mountain peaks rose into the air like two great flames, the whole snow field had turned crimson, and rosy-colored clouds floated in the sky above. The grass upon the mountainsides had turned to gold, the rocks were all aglow, and the whole valley was bathed in golden mist. And as Heidi stood gazing around her at all this splendor the tears ran down her cheeks for very delight and happiness, and impulsively she put her hands together, and lifting her eyes to heaven, thanked God aloud for having brought her home, thanked Him that everything was as beautiful as ever, more beautiful even than she had thought, and that it was all hers again once more. And she was so overflowing with joy and thankfulness that she could not find words to thank Him enough. Not until the glory began to fade could she tear herself away.

Then she ran on so quickly that in a very little while she caught sight of the tops of the fir trees above the hut roof, then the roof itself, and at last the whole hut. There was grandfather sitting as in old days smoking his pipe, and she could see the fir trees waving in the wind. Quicker and quicker went her little feet, and before Alm-Uncle had time to see who was coming Heidi had rushed up to him, thrown down her basket, and flung her arms around his neck, unable in the excitement of seeing him again to say more than "Grandfather! Grandfather! Grandfather!" over and over again.

And the old man himself said nothing. For the first time in many years his eyes were wet, and he had to pass his hand across them. Then he unloosed Heidi's arms, put her on his knee, and after looking at her

for a moment, said, "So you have come back to me,
Heidi. How is that? You don't look much of a
grand lady. Did they send you away?"

"Oh, no, grandfather," said Heidi eagerly, "you
must not think that. They were all so kind—Clara,
and grandmamma, and Mr. Sesemann. But you see,
grandfather, I did not know how to contain myself
till I got home again to you. I used to think I should
die, for I felt as if I could not breathe, but I never
said anything because it would have been ungrateful.
And then suddenly one morning quite early Mr. Sesemann said to me—but I think it was partly the doctor's doing—but perhaps it's all in the letter—" and
Heidi jumped down and brought the package and the
letter and handed them both to her grandfather.

"That belongs to you," said the latter, laying the
package down on the bench beside him. Then he
opened the letter, read it through, and without a word
put it in his pocket.

"Do you think you can still drink milk with me,
Heidi?" he asked, taking the child by the hand.
"Bring your money with you; you can buy a bed
and bedclothes and dresses for a couple of years
with it."

"I am sure I do not want it," replied Heidi. "I
have got a bed already, and Clara has put such a lot
of clothes in my box that I shall never want any more."

"Take it and put it in the cupboard; you will want it someday I have no doubt."

Heidi took up her money and skipped happily after her grandfather into the house. She ran into all the corners, delighted to see everything again, and then went up the ladder. There she came to a pause and called down in a tone of surprise and distress, "Oh, grandfather, my bed's gone."

"We can soon make it up again," he answered her from below. "I did not know that you were coming back. Come along now and have your milk."

Heidi came down, climbed on her high stool in the old place, and then taking up her bowl drank her milk eagerly, as if she had never come across anything so delicious. As she put down her bowl, she exclaimed, "Our milk tastes better than anything else in the world, grandfather."

A shrill whistle was heard outside. Heidi darted out like a flash of lightning. There were the goats leaping and springing down the rocks, with Peter in their midst. When he caught sight of Heidi he stood still with astonishment and gazed speechlessly at her. Heidi called out, "Good evening, Peter," and then ran in among the goats. "Little Swan! Little Bear! Do you know me again?"

The animals evidently recognized her voice at once, for they began rubbing their heads against her and bleating loudly as if for joy, and as she called the other goats by name one after the other, they all came scampering toward her helter-skelter and crowding round her. The impatient Greenfinch sprang into the air and over two of her companions in order to get nearer, and even the shy little Snowflake butted the Great Turk out of her way in quite a determined manner.

Heidi was almost out of her mind with delight at being among her old friends again. She flung her arms round the pretty little Snowflake, stroked the mischievous Greenfinch, while she herself was thrust at from all sides by the affectionate goats. So at last she came near to where Peter was still standing, not yet over his surprise.

"Come down, Peter," cried Heidi, "and say good evening to me."

"So you are back again?" he found words to say at last. He ran down and took Heidi's hand which she was holding out in greeting, and immediately put the same question to her which he had been in the habit of asking in the old days when they returned home in the evening, "Will you come out with me tomorrow?"

"Not tomorrow, but the day after perhaps, for tomorrow I must go down to grandmother."

"I am glad you are back," said Peter, while his whole face beamed with pleasure. He prepared to go on with his goats, but he never had had so much trouble with them before. When at last, by coaxing and threats he had them all together, and Heidi had gone off with an arm around each of her grandfather's two, the whole flock suddenly turned and ran after her. Heidi had to go inside the stall with her two and shut the door or Peter would never have reached home that night.

When Heidi went indoors she found her bed already made up for her. The hay had been piled high for it and smelled delicious. The grandfather had carefully spread and tucked in the clean sheets. It was with a happy heart that Heidi lay down in it that night, and her sleep was sounder than it had been for a whole year past. The grandfather got up at least ten times during the night and mounted the ladder to see if Heidi was all right. But Heidi did not stir; she had no need now to wander about, for the great burning longing of her heart was satisfied. She had seen the high mountains and rocks alight in the evening glow and she had heard the wind in the fir trees. She was at home again on the mountain.

Sunday Bells ⤶

Heidi was standing under the waving fir trees waiting for the grandfather, who was going down with her to grandmother's, and then on to Dörfli to bring up her trunk. It was Saturday, a day when Alm-Uncle made everything clean and neat inside and outside the house. He had devoted the morning to this work so as to be able to accompany Heidi in the afternoon, and the whole place was now as spick and span as he liked to see it. "Well, now we can be off," he called cheerfully as he came out. They parted at the grandmother's cottage, and Heidi ran in. The grandmother had heard her steps approaching and greeted her as she crossed the threshold, "Is it you, child? Have you come again?"

Then she took hold of Heidi's hand and held it fast in her own, for she still seemed to fear that the child might be torn from her again. She had to tell Heidi right away how much she had enjoyed the white bread, and how much stronger it had made her feel already. Brigitta said that she was sure if her

154

mother could eat like that for a week she would get back some of her strength, but she was so afraid of coming to the end of the rolls that she had eaten only one as yet. Heidi listened to all Brigitta said, and sat thinking for a while. Then she suddenly thought of a way.

"I know, grandmother, what I will do," she said eagerly. "I will write to Clara, and she will send me as many rolls again, if not twice as many, as you have now. I had ever such a large heap in the wardrobe, and when they were all taken away she promised to give me as many back, and she would do so I am sure."

"That is a good idea," said Brigitta, "but then, they would get hard and stale. The baker in Dörfli makes the white rolls, but I can only just manage to pay for the black bread."

A further bright thought came to Heidi, and her little face lighted up with joy. "Oh, I have lots of money, grandmother," she cried gleefully, skipping about the room in her delight, "and I know now what I will do with it. You must have a fresh white roll every day, and two on Sunday. Peter can bring them up from Dörfli."

"No, no, child!" answered the grandmother. "I cannot let you do that. The money was not given to you for that purpose. You must give it to your grandfather, and he will tell you how you are to spend it."

But Heidi would not listen. She continued to jump about, saying joyously over and over, "Now, grandmother can have a roll every day and will grow quite strong again. Oh, grandmother" she suddenly exclaimed, still more happily, "if you get strong maybe everything will grow light again for you; perhaps it's only because you are weak that it is dark."

The grandmother said nothing, for she did not wish to spoil the child's pleasure. As Heidi went jumping, about, she suddenly caught sight of the grandmother's songbook, and another happy idea struck her. "Grandmother, I can read now. Would you like me to read you one of your hymns from your old book?"

"Oh, yes," said the grandmother, surprised and delighted. "Can you really read, child, really?"

Heidi had climbed up on a chair and had already lifted down the book, bringing a cloud of dust with it, for it had lain untouched on the shelf for a long time. Heidi wiped it, sat down on a stool beside the old woman, and asked her which hymn she should read.

"What you like, child, what you like." The grandmother pushed her spinning wheel aside and sat eagerly waiting for Heidi to begin. Heidi turned over the leaves and read a line out softly to herself here and there.

At last she said, "Here is one about the sun, grandmother. I will read you that."

The grandmother sat with folded hands and a look

of indescribable joy on her face, such as Heidi had never seen there before although at the same time the tears were running down her cheeks. As Heidi finished, the grandmother begged, "Read it again, just once again."

So Heidi, as pleased as the grandmother, read the hymn again.

"Ah, Heidi, that brings light to the heart! What comfort you have brought me!"

The old woman kept on repeating the glad words, while Heidi beamed with happiness. She could not take her eyes from the grandmother's face, for it had never looked like that before. It had no longer the troubled expression, but was alight with peace and joy as if she were already looking with new, clear eyes into the garden of Paradise.

Someone now knocked at the window and Heidi looked up and saw her grandfather beckoning her to come home with him. As she was going out Brigitta ran to her with the frock and hat she had left. Heidi put the dress over her arm, but she refused to take back the hat.

Heidi could hardly wait to tell her grandfather of her plan to buy rolls for the grandmother. "The money is yours," he said. "Do what you like with it. You can buy bread for grandmother for years to come with it."

Heidi shouted for joy at the thought that grand-

mother would never need to eat hard, black bread
again. "Oh, grandfather!" she said. "Everything is
happier now than it has ever been in our lives before!
If God had let me come at once, as I prayed, then
everything would have been different. I should have
had only a little bread to bring to grandmother, and
I should not have been able to read, which is such a
comfort to her. God has arranged it all so much better than I knew how to. Everything has happened
just as the other grandmother said it would. And
now I shall always pray to God as she told me, and
always thank Him, and when He does not do anything I ask for I shall think to myself, 'It's just as it
was in Frankfurt. God, I am sure, is going to do
something better still.' So we will pray every day,
won't we, grandfather, and never forget Him again?"

"And suppose we do forget Him?" said the grandfather in a low voice.

"Then everything goes wrong, for God lets us then
go where we like. When we get poor and miserable
and begin to cry about it no one pities us, but everyone says, 'You ran away from God, and so God, who
could have helped you, left you to yourself!'"

"That is true, Heidi, where did you learn it?"

"From grandmamma. She explained it all to me."

The grandfather walked on for a little while with
out speaking, then he said, as if following his own
train of thought: "And if it is so once, it is so always.

No one can go back, and he whom God has forgotten, is forgotten forever."

"Oh, no, grandfather, we can go back, for grandmamma told me so, and so it was in the beautiful tale in my book. You have not heard that yet, but I will read it to you as soon as we get home."

When they reached the hut the old man sat down on the bench. Heidi soon came running out with her book under her arm. In a second she was beside him had her book open. In a sympathetic voice Heidi began to read of the Prodigal Son when he was happily at home, and went out into the fields with his father's flocks. The picture showed him dressed in a fine cloak, watching the sunset.

But then all at once he wanted to have his own goods and money and to be his own master, and so he asked his father to give him his share, and he left his home and went and wasted all his money. And when he had nothing left he hired himself out to a master who had no flocks and fields such as his father had, but only swine to keep. So the young man was obliged to watch these, and he had only rags to wear and a few husks to eat such as the swine fed upon.

Then he thought of his old happy life at home and how kindly his father had treated him and how ungrateful he had been, and he wept for sorrow and longing. And he thought to himself, "I will arise and go to my father, and will say to him, 'Father, I am not worthy to be called thy son; make me as one of thy hired servants.' " And when he was yet a great way off his father saw him . . .

Here Heidi paused in her reading. "What do you think happens now, grandfather?" she said. "Do you think the father is angry and will say to him, 'I told you so'? Well, listen.

" 'His father saw him, and had compassion, and ran, and fell on his neck and kissed him. And the son said to him, "Father, I have sinned against heaven and in thy sight, and am no more worthy to be called thy son." But the father said to his servants, "Bring forth the best robe, and put it on him; and put a ring on his hand and shoes on his feet; and bring hither the fatted calf and kill it; and let us eat and be merry, for this my son was dead and is alive again; he was lost and is found." And they began to be merry.'

"Isn't that a beautiful story, grandfather?" asked Heidi as the old man sat without speaking. She was surprised that he had not expressed pleasure and astonishment.

"You are right, Heidi; it is a beautiful story," he replied, but he looked so grave as he said it that Heidi grew silent herself and sat looking quietly at her pictures.

A few hours later, as Heidi lay fast asleep in her bed, the grandfather went up the ladder and put his lamp down near her bed, so that the light fell on the sleeping child. Her hands were still folded as if she had fallen asleep saying her prayers, and an expression of peace and trust lay on the little face. The grandfather stood for a long time gazing down at her.

At last he too folded his hands, and with bowed head said in a low voice, "Father, I have sinned against heaven and before thee and am not worthy to be called thy son." And two large tears rolled down the old man's cheeks.

Early the next morning he stood in front of his hut and gazed around him. The fresh, bright, morning sun lay on mountain and valley. The sound of a few early bells floated up from the valley, and the birds were singing their morning song in the fir trees. He stepped back into the hut and called up, "Come along, Heidi! The sun is up! Put on your best frock, for we are going to church together!"

Heidi was not long getting ready. It was such an unusual summons from her grandfather that she had to hurry. She put on her smart Frankfurt dress and soon went down, but when she saw her grandfather she stood still, gazing at him in astonishment. "Why, grandfather!" she exclaimed. "I never saw you look like that before! I never saw that coat with the silver buttons! Oh, you do look fine in your Sunday coat!"

The old man smiled and replied, "So do you look fine. Now come along!" He took Heidi's hand in

his and together they walked down the mountainside.
The bells were ringing in every direction now, sound-
ing louder and fuller as they neared the valley, and
Heidi listened to them with delight. "Listen to them,
grandfather! It's like a great festival."

The congregation had already assembled and the
singing had begun when Heidi and her grandfather entered the church at Dörfli and sat down at the back.
But before the hymn was over everyone was nudging
his neighbor and whispering, "Do you see? Alm-
Uncle is in church!"

At the close of the service Alm-Uncle took Heidi
by the hand, and together they went toward the pastor's house. The rest of the congregation looked
curiously after them. Some even followed until they
saw them go inside the pastor's house. Then they
collected in groups and talked over this strange event.

Meanwhile Alm-Uncle had gone into the pastor's
house and knocked at the study door. The pastor
shook hands warmly with him, and Alm-Uncle was
unable at first to speak, for he had not expected such
a friendly reception.

At last he collected himself and said: "I have come
to ask you, pastor, to forget the words I spoke to you
when you called on me, and to beg you not to feel any
ill will toward me for having been so stubbornly set
against your well-meant advice. You were right, and
I was wrong, but I have now made up my mind to

follow your advice. I am going to find a place for
myself at Dörfli for the winter, for the child is not
strong enough to stand the bitter cold up on the
mountain. And if the people down here look askance
at me, as at a person not to be trusted, I know it is my
own fault, and you will, I am sure, not do so."

The pastor's kindly eyes shone with pleasure. He
pressed the old man's hand in his, and said with emotion, "Neighbor, I am very glad. You will not be
sorry, I am sure, that you decided to come live with
us again. You will always be welcome here as a dear
friend and neighbor, and I look forward to our
spending many a pleasant winter evening together.
We will find some friends, too, for the little one."
And the pastor laid his hand kindly on the child's
curly head, and took her by the hand as he walked
to the door with the old man. He did not say good-by
to him till they were outside, so that all the people
standing about saw him shake hands as if he were
parting reluctantly from his best friend.

The door had hardly shut behind him before the
whole congregation came forward to greet Alm-
Uncle. Everyone was trying to be the first to shake
hands with him, and so many hands were held out
that Alm-Uncle did not know which to grasp first.
When Alm-Uncle told them he was thinking of returning to his old quarters in Dörfli for the winter,
there was such a general chorus of pleasure that any-

one would have thought he was the most beloved person in all Dörfli, and that they had hardly known how to live without him.

Most of his friends accompanied him and Heidi some way up the mountain, and each as they bade him good-by made him promise that when he next came down he would without fail come and call. As the old man at last stood alone with the child, watching their retreating figures, there was a light upon his face as if reflected from some inner sunshine of heart.

Heidi looked up at him with her clear, steady eyes and said, "Grandfather, you look happier and happier today. I never saw you quite like that before."

"Do you think so?" he said with a smile. "Well, yes, Heidi, I am happier today than I deserve, happier than I had thought possible. It is good to be at peace with God and man! God was good to me when he sent you to my hut."

When they reached Peter's home the grandfather opened the door and walked straight in. "Good morning, grandmother," he said. "I think we shall have to do some more patching up before the autumn winds come."

"Dear God, if it is not Uncle!" cried the grandmother in pleased surprise. "That I should live to see such a thing! And now I can thank you for all that you have done for me. May God reward you! May God reward you!" She stretched out a trembling hand to him, and when the grandfather shook it warmly, she went on, still holding his, "And I have something on my heart I want to say, a prayer to make to you! If I have injured you in any way, do not punish me by sending the child away again before I lie under the grass. Oh, you do not know what the child is to me!" And she clasped the child to her, for Heidi had already taken her usual stand close to the grandmother.

"Have no fear, grandmother," said Uncle in a re-assuring voice, "I shall not punish either you or myself by doing so. We are all together now, and pray God we may continue so for long."

Brigitta now drew the Uncle aside toward a corner of the room and showed him the hat with the feathers, explaining to him how it came there, and adding that of course she could not take such a thing from the child.

But the grandfather looked at Heidi without any displeasure and said, "The hat is hers, and if she does not wish to wear it any more she has a right to say so and to give it to you. So take it, pray."

Brigitta was highly delighted.

At this moment Peter rushed in. He had a letter for Heidi which had been delivered at the post office in Dörfli.

They all sat down round the table to hear what was in it, for Heidi opened it at once and read it without hesitation. The letter was from Clara. She wrote that the house had been so dull since Heidi left that she did not know how to endure it. She had at last persuaded her father to take her to the baths at Ragatz in the coming autumn. Grandmamma had arranged to join them there, and they both were looking forward to paying her and her grandfather a visit. And grandmamma sent a further message to Heidi that she had done quite right to take the rolls to the grandmother, and so that she might not have to eat them dry, she was sending some coffee. Grandmamma hoped when she came to the Alm in the autumn that Heidi would take her to see her old friend.

There were exclamations of pleasure and astonishment on hearing all this news, and so much to talk and ask about that the minutes flew. All too soon it was time for the grandfather and Heidi to start up the mountain.

"You will come soon again, Uncle, and you, child, tomorrow?" begged the grandmother.

The old man and Heidi promised her faithfully to do so. As they had been greeted with bells when they made their journey down in the morning, so now they were accompanied by the peaceful evening chimes as they climbed to the hut.

Preparations for a Journey ∽

THE kind doctor who had given the order that Heidi was to be sent home was walking along one of the broad streets toward Mr. Sesemann's house. It was a sunny September morning, so full of light and sweetness that it seemed as if everybody must rejoice. But the doctor walked with his eyes on the ground. There was an expression of sadness on his face, formerly so cheerful, and his hair had grown grayer since the spring. The doctor had had an only daughter, who, after his wife's death, had been his constant companion. She had died only a few months before and he had never been able to look bright and cheery since.

"I am glad you have come, doctor," exclaimed Mr. Sesemann as his friend entered. "We must really have another talk about this Swiss journey. Do you still stick to your decision, even though Clara is decidedly improving in health?"

"My dear Sesemann, I never knew such a man as you!" said the doctor as he sat down beside his friend. "I really wish your mother were here. Everything would be clear and straightforward then and she would soon have things straightened out. You sent for me three times yesterday only to ask me the same question, though you know what I think."

"Yes, I know it's enough to make you out of patience with me; but you must understand, dear friend"—and Mr. Sesemann laid his hand imploringly on the doctor's shoulder—"that I feel I have not the courage to refuse the child what I have been promising her all along. For months now she has been living on the thought of it day and night. She bore this last bad attack so patiently because she was buoyed up with the hope that she should soon start on her Swiss journey and see her friend Heidi again. Now must I tell the poor child, who has to give up so many pleasures, that this visit she has so long looked forward to must also be canceled? I really have not the courage to do it."

"You must make up your mind to it, Sesemann," said the doctor with authority. As his friend sat silent and dejected he went on after a pause, "Consider yourself how the matter stands. Clara has not had such a bad summer as this last one for years. Only the worst results would follow from the fatigue of such a journey, and it is out of the question for her. But I will go in with you and talk to Clara. She is a reasonable child, and I will tell her what my plans are. Next May she shall be taken to the baths and stay there for the cure until it is quite hot weather. Then she can be carried up the mountain from time to time, and when she is stronger she will enjoy these excursions far more than she would now. If we want to give the child a chance of recovery we must use the utmost care and watchfulness."

Mr. Sesemann, who had listened to the doctor in sad and submissive silence, now suddenly jumped up. "Doctor," he said, "tell me truly. Have you really any hope of her final recovery?"

The doctor shrugged his shoulders. "Very little," he replied quietly. "But, friend, think of my trouble. You have still a beloved child to look for you and greet you on your return home. You do not come back to an empty house and sit down to a solitary meal. And the child is happy and comfortable at home, too. If there is much that she has to give up, she has, on the other hand, many advantages. No, Sesemann, you are not so greatly to be pitied—you still have the happiness of being together. Think of my lonely house!"

Mr. Sesemann was now striding up and down the room as was his habit when he was deeply engaged in thought. Suddenly he came to a pause beside his friend and laid his hand on his shoulder. "Doctor, I have an idea. I cannot bear to see you look as you do; you are no longer the same man. You must be taken out of yourself for a while. I propose that you

take the journey and go and pay Heidi a visit in our
name."

The doctor was taken aback at this sudden proposal
and wanted to make objections, but his friend gave
him no time to say anything. He was so delighted
with his idea that he seized the doctor by the arm
and drew him into Clara's room. The kind doctor
was always a welcome visitor to Clara. Lately, it is
true, he had been graver, but Clara knew why and
would have given much to see him his old lively self
again.

She held out her hand to him as he came up to her
and took a seat beside her. Her father also drew up
his chair, and taking Clara's hand in his began to talk
to her of the Swiss journey and how he himself had
looked forward to it. He passed as quickly as he
could over the main point that it was now impossible
for her to undertake it, for he dreaded the tears that
would follow. Without pause he went on to tell her
of his new plan. He emphasized the great benefit it
would be to the doctor if he could be persuaded to
take this holiday.

The tears were indeed swimming in the blue eyes,
although Clara struggled to keep them down for her
father's sake. She knew that he would never refuse
her a thing unless he was certain that it would be
harmful for her. So she swallowed her tears and
taking the doctor's hand she said pleadingly:

"Dear doctor, you will go and see Heidi, won't you? Then you can come and tell me all about it, what it is like up there, and what Heidi and the grandfather, and Peter and the goats do all day. I know them all so well! And then you can take what I want to send to Heidi. Do go, dear doctor, and I will take as much cod-liver oil as you like."

Whether this promise finally decided the doctor it is impossible to say, but it is certain that he smiled and said: "Then I must certainly go, Clara, for if you do that you will get as plump and strong as your father and I wish to see you. And have you decided when I am to start?"

"Tomorrow morning—early if possible," replied Clara.

"Yes, she is right," put in Mr. Sesemann. "The sun is shining and the sky is blue, and there is no time to be lost. It is a pity to miss a single one of these days on the mountain."

The doctor could not help laughing. "You will be reproaching me next for not being there already! Well, I must go and make arrangements for getting off."

But Clara would not let him go until she had given him endless messages for Heidi. Her presents she would send round later, when Miss Rottenmeier had packed them.

At the street door the doctor met with a sudden obstacle. Miss Rottenmeier was returning from a

walk and reached the door just as he did. The white
shawl she wore was so blown out by the wind that
she looked like a ship in full sail. The doctor drew
back, but Miss Rottenmeier had always shown peculiar appreciation and respect for this man, and she
also drew back with exaggerated politeness to let him
pass.

The two stood for a few seconds, each anxious
to make way for the other, but a sudden gust of wind
sent Miss Rottenmeier flying with all her sails almost
into the doctor's arms, and she had to pause and recover herself before she could shake hands with the
doctor with becoming decorum. She was annoyed
because she had been forced to enter in so undignified
a manner, but the doctor had a way of smoothing
people's ruffled feathers, and she was soon listening
with her usual composure while he informed her of
his intended journey. He begged her in his most
agreeable manner to pack up the parcels for Heidi
as she alone knew how to pack. And then he took
his leave.

Clara quite expected to have a long tussle with Miss
Rottenmeier before the housekeeper would consent
to send all the things that she had collected as presents
for Heidi. But this time she was mistaken, for Miss
Rottenmeier was in an unusually good temper. She
cleared the large table so that all the things for Heidi
could be spread out upon it and packed under Clara's

own eyes. It was no light job, for the presents were of all shapes and sizes. First there was a little warm cloak with a hood, which had been designed by Clara herself, in order that Heidi during the coming winter might be able to go and see grandmother when she liked. Then came a thick, warm shawl for the grandmother, in which she could wrap herself up well and not feel the cold when the wind came sweeping in such terrible gusts round the house.

The next object was a large box full of cakes. These were also for the grandmother, that she might have something to eat with her coffee besides bread. An immense sausage for Peter's mother was the next article.

A packet of tobacco was a present for grandfather, who was so fond of his pipe as he sat resting in the evening. Finally there were a whole lot of mysterious little bags and parcels and boxes which Clara had had especial pleasure in collecting, for each was to be a joyful surprise for Heidi as she opened it. The work came to an end at last, and an imposing-looking package lay ready on the floor. Clara eyed it with pleasure, picturing Heidi's exclamations and jumps of joy and surprise when the huge parcel arrived at the hut.

Sebastian came in, and lifting the package up on his shoulder, carried it off to be forwarded at once to the doctor's house.

THE early light of morning lay rosy red upon the mountains, and a fresh breeze rustled through the fir trees and set their ancient branches waving to and fro. The sound awoke Heidi and she opened her eyes. The roaring in the trees always stirred a strong emotion within her and seemed to draw her irresistibly to them. So she jumped out of bed and dressed as quickly as she could.

When she went down the ladder she found that her grandfather had already left the hut. He was standing outside looking at the sky and examining the landscape as he did every morning, to see what sort of weather it was going to be.

Little pink clouds were floating over the sky, that was growing brighter and bluer with every minute. The heights and the meadowlands were turning gold under the rising sun, which was just appearing above the topmost peaks.

"O how beautiful! How beautiful! Good morning, grandfather!" cried Heidi, running out.

174

"What, you are awake already, are you?" he answered, giving her a morning greeting.

Then Heidi ran round to the fir trees to enjoy the sound she loved so well, and with every fresh gust of wind which came roaring through their branches she gave a fresh jump and cry of delight.

Meanwhile the grandfather had gone to milk Little Swan. This done, he brushed and washed the goats, ready for their mountain excursion, and brought them out of their shed. As soon as Heidi caught sight of her two friends she ran and embraced them. They bleated in return, and vied with each other in showing their affection by poking their heads against her and trying to see which could get nearest her, so that she was almost crushed between them.

And now Peter's whistle was heard, and all the goats came along, leaping and springing. Heidi soon found herself surrounded by the whole flock, pushed this way and that by their rough greetings, but at last she managed to get through them to where Snowflake was standing, for the young goat had tried in vain to reach her.

Peter now gave a last tremendous whistle, in order to startle the goats and drive them off, for he himself wanted to get near to say something to Heidi. The goats sprang aside and he came up to her.

"Can you come out with me today?" he asked, evidently unwilling to hear her refuse.

"I am afraid I cannot, Peter," she answered. "I am expecting the folks every minute from Frankfurt, and I must be at home when they come."

"You have said the same thing for days now," grumbled Peter.

"I must keep on saying it till they come," replied Heidi. "How can you think, Peter, that I would be away when they came? As if I could do such a thing!"

"They would find Uncle at home," he answered crossly.

But at this moment the grandfather's deep voice was heard. "Why is the army not marching forward? Is it the field marshal who is missing or some of the troops?"

Peter immediately turned and went off, swinging his stick around so that it whistled through the air. The goats understood the signal and started at full trot for their mountain pasture.

Since Heidi had been back with her grandfather she thought of things that had never occurred to her before. With great exertion, she put her bed in order every morning, patting and stroking it till she had got it perfectly smooth and flat. Then she went about the room downstairs, put each chair back in its place, and if she found anything lying about she put it in the cupboard. After that she brought a duster, climbed on a chair, and rubbed the table till it shone again.

When the grandfather came in later he would look round well pleased and say to himself: "We look like Sunday every day now. Heidi did not go away for nothing."

This morning, after Peter had departed and Heidi and her grandfather had breakfasted, the little girl began her daily work as usual, but she did not get on with it very fast. It was so lovely out-of-doors that she felt she could not stay inside. The sunlight lay sparkling on everything around the hut and on all the mountains and far away along the valley, and the grass slope looked so golden and inviting that she was obliged to sit down for a few minutes and look about her.

Then she remembered her unfinished duties and jumped up and ran inside. But it was not long before the fir trees began their old song, and Heidi was off to play and leap to the tune of the waving branches. The grandfather, who was busy in his work shed, stepped out from time to time, smiling to watch her at her play. He had just gone back to his work on one of these occasions when Heidi called out, "Grandfather! Grandfather! Come! Come!"

He stepped quickly out, almost afraid something had happened to the child, but he saw her running down the path, crying, "They are coming! They are coming! And the doctor is in front of them!"

When Heidi reached her old friend she clung to his

outstretched arm, and exclaimed in the joy of her heart, "Good morning, doctor, and thank you ever so many times."

"God bless you, child! What have you to thank me for?" asked the doctor, smiling.

"For being at home again with grandfather," the child explained.

The doctor's face brightened as if a sudden ray of sunshine had passed across it. He had not expected such a reception as this. He had quite thought that Heidi would have forgotten him; she had seen so little of him. He had felt, too, rather like one bearing a message of disappointment, coming as he did without the expected friends. But here was Heidi, her eyes dancing for joy, clinging affectionately to his arm and pouring out her thanks to him.

He took her by the hand with fatherly tenderness. "Take me now to your grandfather, Heidi, and show me where you live."

But Heidi still remained standing looking down the path with questioning gaze. "Where are Clara and grandmother?" she asked.

"Ah, now I have to tell you something which you will be as sorry about as I am," answered the doctor. "You see, Heidi, I have come alone. Clara was very ill and could not travel, and so the grandmother stayed behind, too. But next spring, when the days grow warm and long again, they are coming here for certain."

Heidi was sorely disappointed. She could not at first bring herself to believe that what she had for so long been picturing to herself was not going to happen after all. She stood motionless for a second or two, overcome by the unexpected disappointment. Then she suddenly remembered that the doctor had really come. She lifted her eyes and saw the sad expression in his as he looked down at her. She had never seen him with that look on his face when she was in Frankfurt. It went to Heidi's heart. She could not bear to see anybody unhappy, especially her dear doctor. No doubt it was because Clara and grandmother could not come, and so she began to think how best she might console him.

"Oh, it won't be very long to wait for spring, and then they will be sure to come," she said in a reassuring voice. "Time passes very quickly with us, and then they will be able to stay longer when they are here, and Clara will be pleased at that. Now let us go and find grandfather."

Hand in hand with her friend she climbed up to the hut. She was so anxious to make the doctor happy again that she began once more assuring him that the winter passed so quickly on the mountain that it was hardly to be taken account of, and that summer would be back again before they knew it. She became so convinced of the truth of her own words that she called out quite cheerfully to her grandfather as they approached, "They have not come today, but they will be here in a very short time."

The doctor was no stranger to the grandfather, for the child had talked to him so much about her friend. The old man held out his hand to his guest in friendly greeting. Then they all three sat down in front of the hut. The doctor whispered to Heidi that there was something being brought up the mountain which had traveled with him from Frankfurt, and which would give her even more pleasure than seeing the old doctor. Heidi got into a great state of excitement on hearing this, wondering what it could be.

The old man urged the doctor to spend as many of the beautiful autumn days on the mountain as he could. He advised him not to go back to Ragatz, but to stay at Dörfli, where there was a clean, neat, little inn. Then he could come up every morning, and, if he liked, the grandfather would act as his guide to any part of the mountains he would like to see. The doctor was delighted with this proposal.

It was now noon. The wind had sunk and the fir trees stood motionless. The air was still wonderfully warm and mild for that height, while a delicious freshness was mingled with the warmth of the sun.

Alm-Uncle rose and went indoors, returning in a few minutes with a table which he placed in front of the seat.

"There, Heidi, now run in and bring us what we

want for the table," he said. "The doctor must take us as he finds us. If the food is plain, he will acknowledge that the dining room is pleasant."

"I should think so, indeed," replied the doctor as he looked down over the sun-lit valley. "Everything must taste good up here."

Heidi ran back and forth, delighted that she could help to entertain the doctor. The grandfather now appeared with a steaming jug of milk and golden-brown toasted cheese and some thin slices of meat he had cured. The doctor enjoyed his dinner better than he had for a year.

"Our Clara must certainly come up here," he said. "'It would make her quite a different person, and if she ate for any length of time as I have today, she would grow plumper than anyone has ever know her before."

As he spoke a man was seen coming up the path, carrying a large package on his back. When he reached the top he threw his load on the ground and drew in two or three good breaths of the mountain air.

"Ah, here's what traveled with me from Frankfurt," said the doctor, rising, and he went up to the package and began undoing it. Heidi looked on in great expectation. After he had released it from its heavy outer covering, "There, child," he said, "now you can go on unpacking your treasures yourself."

Heidi opened her presents one by one until they were all displayed. She could not speak for wonder and delight. Not till the doctor went up to her again and opened the large box to show Heidi the cakes that were for the grandmother to eat with her coffee, did she at last give a cry of joy, exclaiming, "Now grandmother will have nice things to eat!" She wanted to pack everything up again and start at once to give them to her. But the grandfather said he would walk down with the doctor that evening and she could go with them then and take the things.

Heidi now found the packet of tobacco which she ran and gave to her grandfather. He was so pleased with it that he immediately filled his pipe with some, and the two men sat together, the smoke curling up from their pipes as they talked of all kinds of things. Heidi continued to examine first one and then another of her presents. Suddenly she ran up to the men, and standing in front of the doctor waited till there was a pause in the conversation, and then said, "No, the other thing has not given me more pleasure than seeing you, doctor."

The two men could not help laughing, and the doctor answered that he should never have thought it possible.

As the sun began to sink behind the mountains the doctor rose, thinking it time to return to Dörfli and hunt for lodgings. The grandfather carried the cakes

and the shawl and the large sausage, and the doctor
took Heidi's hand and they all three started down the
mountain. When they reached Peter's home Heidi
bade the others good-by. She was to wait at grandmother's till her grandfather, who was going on to
Dörfli with his guest returned for her. As the doctor
shook hands with her she asked, "Would you like to
come out with the goats tomorrow morning?" for
she could think of no greater treat to offer him.

"Agreed!" answered the doctor. "We will go together."

The grandfather put the presents down by the door,
and with some effort Heidi managed to carry in the
box of cakes. Then she ran out again and brought
in the sausage. The third time she brought the shawl.
She placed them as close as she could to the grandmother, so that the old woman might be able to feel
them and understand what was there. The shawl she
laid over the grandmother's knees.

"They are all from Frankfurt, from Clara and
grandmamma," she explained to the astonished grandmother and Brigitta.

"And you are very pleased with the cakes, aren't
you, grandmother? Taste how soft they are!" said
Heidi over and over again, to which the grandmother
continued to answer, "Yes, yes, Heidi, I should think
so! What kind people they must be!" She passed
her hand over the warm, thick shawl and added:

"This will be beautiful for the cold weather! I never thought I should have such a splendid thing as this to put on."

Heidi could not help feeling some surprise that the grandmother seemed to take more pleasure in the shawl than in the cakes.

Peter came tumbling in at this minute. "Uncle is just behind me, he is coming—" he began, and then stopped short, for he had caught sight of the sausage, and he was too much taken aback to say more. But Heidi understood that her grandfather was near and so said good-by to grandmother. The old man now never passed the door without going in to wish the grandmother good day, but it was late this evening so he only called good night through the open door and together he and Heidi climbed under the starlit sky back to their peaceful home.

A Compensation ❧

T HE next morning the doctor climbed up from
Dörfli with Peter and the goats. The kindly
gentleman tried now and then to enter into conversation with the boy, but his attempts failed, for he
could hardly get a word out of Peter in answer to his
questions. At the hut they found Heidi waiting with
her two goats.

The grandfather now came out with the dinner
bag, and after bidding good day to the doctor he went
up to Peter and slung it over his neck. It was heavier
than usual, for Alm-Uncle had added some meat
today.

As they started, the goats came thronging around
Heidi, but by degrees she managed to make her way
out from among them and joined the doctor, who took
her by the hand. Heidi had a great deal to say about
the goats and their peculiarities, and about the flowers
and the rocks and the birds. So they clambered on
and reached their resting place before they knew it.

185

Peter had sent a good many unfriendly glances toward the doctor on the way up.

Heidi now led her friend to her favorite spot. Over the heights and over the far green valley hung the golden glory of the autumn day. Overhead the great bird was flying round and round in wide circles, but today he made no sound. The doctor sat thoughtfully gazing around him.

"Heidi," he said slowly, "it is beautiful here, but tell me—if we bring sad hearts up here, how may they be healed so that we can rejoice in all this beauty?"

"Oh, but," exclaimed Heidi, "no one is sad up here, only in Frankfurt."

The doctor smiled, and then growing serious again he continued, "But supposing we are not able to leave all the sadness behind at Frankfurt. Can you tell me anything that will help then?"

"When we do not know what more to do we must go and tell everything to God," answered Heidi with decision.

"Ah, that is a good thought of yours, Heidi," said the doctor. "But if it is God Himself who has sent the trouble, what can we say to Him then?"

Heidi sat thinking for a while.

"Then we must wait," she said, "and keep on saying to ourselves, 'God certainly knows of some happiness for us which He is going to bring out of the trouble,

only we must have patience and not run away.' And
then all at once something happens and we see clearly
ourselves that God has had some good thought in His
mind all along; but because we cannot see things beforehand, and only know how dreadfully miserable
we are, we think it is always going to be so."

"That is a beautiful faith, child, and be sure you
hold it fast," replied the doctor. Then he sat on a
while in silence, looking at the great overshadowing
mountains and the green, sunlit valley below before
he spoke again.

"Can you understand, Heidi, that a man may sit
here with such a shadow over his eyes that he cannot
feel and enjoy the beauty around him, while the heart
grows doubly sad knowing how beautiful it could be?
Can you understand that?"

Then in a grave voice she said: "Yes, I can understand it. And I know this, that then one must say one
of grandmother's hymns. They bring the light back a
little, and often make it so bright for her that she is
quite happy again. Grandmother herself told me
this."

"Which hymns are they, Heidi?" asked the doctor.

"I know only the one about the sun and the beautiful garden, and some of the verses of the long one.
They are favorites with her, and she always likes me
to read them to her two or three times over," replied
Heidi.

"Well, say the verses to me then, I should like to hear them, too," said the doctor.

Heidi began to recite the comforting verses.

Suddenly she paused. She was not sure that the doctor was still listening. He was sitting motionless with his hand before his eyes. She thought he had fallen asleep, and sat very quiet. The doctor sat in silence, but he certainly was not asleep. His thoughts had carried him back to a long-past time. He saw himself as a little boy standing by his dear mother's chair. She had her arm around his neck and was saying the very verses to him that Heidi had just recited. He could hear his mother's voice and see her loving eyes resting upon him. When at last he roused himself he met Heidi's eyes looking wonderingly at him.

"Heidi," he said, taking the child's hand in his, "that was a beautiful hymn of yours," and there was a happier ring in his voice as he spoke. "We will come out here together another day, and you will let me hear it again."

Peter was very angry. It was now some days since Heidi had been out with him, and when at last she did come, there she sat the whole time beside the old gentleman. He worked himself into a terrible temper.

Meanwhile the sun had risen to the height which Peter knew pointed to the dinner hour. All of a sudden he called at the top of his voice, "It's dinnertime."

The doctor and Heidi decided they wanted only milk. Peter seemed hardly to understand. "Who is going to eat what is in the bag, then?" he asked.

"You may have it," Heidi answered. "Only first make haste and get the milk."

Peter had seldom performed any task more promptly, for he thought of the bag and its contents, which now belonged to him. As soon as the other two were sitting quietly drinking their milk, he opened the bag. He quite trembled for joy at the sight of the meat, for he was not used to that delicacy.

Heidi and the doctor climbed and talked for a long while, until the doctor said it was time for him to be going back. He wanted Heidi to stay there, but she would not hear to this, for then the doctor would have to go the whole way down the mountain alone. She insisted on going with him as far as the grandfather's hut, or even a little farther. She kept hold of her friend's hand all the time, and the whole way she entertained him with accounts of this thing and that, showing him the spots where the goats liked best to feed, and other places where in summer the flowers of all colors grew in greatest abundance.

At last the doctor insisted on her going back. They bade each other good night and the doctor continued his descent, turning now and again to look back. Each time he saw Heidi standing on the same spot and waving her hand to him. Even so in the old days had his own dear little daughter watched him when he went from home.

It was a bright, sunny, autumn month. The doctor came up the hut every morning, and from there made excursions with Alm-Uncle over the mountain. They climbed up to the ancient, storm-beaten fir trees and often disturbed the great bird, which rose startled from its nest, with a whir of wings and croakings, very near their heads. Alm-Uncle knew the uses of all the plants. He was as well versed also in the ways of the animals, great and small, and had many amusing anecdotes to tell of these dwellers in caves and holes and in the tops of the fir trees. And so the time passed pleasantly and quickly for the doctor. He seldom said good-by to the old man at the end of the day without adding, "I never leave you, friend, without having learned something new from you."

On some of the very finest days, however, the doctor would wander out again with Heidi, and then the two would sit together as on the first day, and the child would repeat her hymns and talk to the doctor.

September had drawn to its close, and now one morning the doctor appeared, looking less cheerful than usual. It was his last day, he said, for he must return to Frankfurt. He was grieved at having to say good-by to the mountain, which had begun to feel quite like home. Alm-Uncle, on his side, greatly regretted the departure of his guest, and Heidi had been now accustomed for so long to seeing her good friend every day that she could hardly believe the time had suddenly come to separate.

He bade farewell to the old man and asked that Heidi might go with him part of the return way. Heidi took his hand and went down the mountain with him, still unable to grasp the idea that he was going for good. After some distance the doctor stood still, and passing his hand over the child's curly head said, "Now, Heidi, you must go back, and I must say good-by! If only I could take you with me to Frankfurt and keep you there!"

The picture of Frankfurt rose before the child's eyes, its rows of endless houses, its hard streets, and even the vision of Miss Rottenmeier and Tinette, and she answered hesitatingly, "I would rather that you came back to us."

"Yes, you are right, that would better. But now good-by, Heidi." The child put her hand in his and looked up at him; the kind eyes looking down on her had tears in them. Then the doctor quickly continued his descent.

Heidi remained standing perfectly still. The sight of the friendly eyes with the tears in them had gone to her heart. All at once she burst into tears and started running as fast as she could after the departing figure, calling out in broken tones: "Doctor! Doctor!"

He turned and waited till the child reached him. The tears were streaming down her face and she sobbed out, "I will come to Frankfurt with you, now at once, and I will stay with you as long as you like, only I must just run back and tell grandfather."

The doctor laid his hand on her head and tried to calm her excitement. "No, no, dear child," he said kindly, "not now. You must stay for the present under the fir trees, or I should have you ill again. But if I am ever ill and alone, will you come then and stay with me? May I know that there would then be someone to look after me and care for me?"

"Yes, yes, I will come the very day you send for me, and I love you nearly as much as grandfather," replied Heidi, who had not yet got over her distress.

And so the doctor again bade her good-by and started on his way, while Heidi remained looking after him and waving her hand has long as she could see him. As the doctor turned for the last time and looked back at the waving Heidi and the sunny mountain, he said to himself, "It is good to be up there, good for body and soul. There a man might learn how to be happy once more."

Winter In Dörfli ꙅ

T HE snow was lying so high around the hut that
the windows looked level with the ground, and
the door had entirely disappeared from view. If
Alm-Uncle had been up there he would have had to do
what Peter did daily, for fresh snow fell every night.
Peter had to get out of the window of the sitting room
every morning. If the frost had not been very hard
during the night, he immediately sank up to his shoulders in the snow and had to struggle with hands, feet,
and head to free himself. Then his mother handed
him the large broom, and with this he worked hard to
make a way to the door. He had to be careful to dig
the snow well away, or else as soon as the door was
opened the whole soft mass would fall inside. If Peter had not cleared away the snow each day a severe
frost would have made such a wall of ice in front of
the house that no one could have gone in or out.

Alm-Uncle had kept his word and was not spending the winter in his old home. As soon as the first
snow began to fall he had shut up the hut and the
outside buildings and gone down to Dörfli with Heidi
and the goats. Near the church was a straggling,
half-ruined building, which had once been the house
of a person of consequence. One of the men of
Dörfli had gone to fight in Spain and had there performed many brave deeds and gathered much treasure.
When he returned to Dörfli he spent part of his
money in building a fine house, with the intention of
living in it. But he had been too long accustomed
to the noise and bustle of arms and the world to care
for a quiet country life, and he soon went off again,
and this time did not return.

When after many long years it seemed certain that
he was dead, a distant relative took possession of the
house, but it was already badly in need of repair, and
he had no wish to rebuild it. So it was let to poor
people, who paid but a small rent, and when any
part of the building fell it was not rebuilt. As long
ago as when his son Tobias was a child Alm-Uncle
had rented the tumbledown old place. Since then
it had stood empty, for no one could stay in it who
had not some idea how to stop up the holes and gaps
and make it comfortable. Otherwise the wind and
rain and snow blew into the rooms, so that it was
impossible even to keep a candle lighted. Anyone

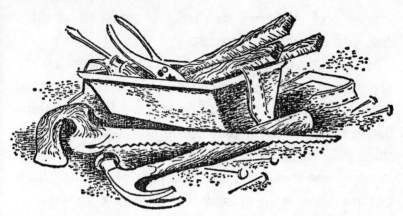

who had tried to live there would have been frozen
to death during the long, cold winters.

Alm-Uncle, however, knew how to fix things up.
As soon as he had made up his mind to spend the
winter in Dörfli, he rented the old place and worked
during the autumn to get it sound and tight. In the
middle of October he and Heidi moved down there.

In the back of the house in what had been a large
hall Uncle had put up a wooden partition and covered the floor with straw. This was to be the goat's
house. Endless passages led from this. Through the
holes in the walls of these passages the sky and the
fields and the road outside could be seen at intervals.
At last one came to a stout oak door leading into a
room that still stood intact. Here the walls and the
dark wainscoting remained as good as ever. In the
corner was an immense stove reaching nearly to the
ceiling. It was covered with white tiles on which
were painted large pictures in blue. There was a

seat around the stove so that one could sit at one's
ease and study the pictures.

These attracted Heidi's attention as soon as she
and her grandfather arrived and she ran and seated
herself and began to examine them. But when she
had gradually worked herself round to the back, something else attracted her attention. In the large space
between the stove and the wall four planks had been
put together as if to make a large box for apples.
There were no apples, inside, however, but something Heidi had no difficulty in recognizing, for it
was her very own bed, with its hay mattress and its
sheets, and the sack for a coverlet, just as she had it
up at the hut.

Heidi clapped her hands for joy and exclaimed,
"Oh, grandfather, this is my room. How nice! But
where are you going to sleep?"

"Your bed must be near the stove or you will
freeze," he replied. "You may come see my room
if you want to."

Heidi got down and skipped across the large room
after her grandfather. He opened a door at the farther end leading into a smaller room which was to
be his bedroom. Then came another door. Heidi
pushed it open and stood amazed, for here was an
immense room like a kitchen, larger than anything
of the kind that Heidi had seen before. There was

still plenty of work for the grandfather before this
room could be finished, for there were holes and
cracks in the walls through which the wind whistled.
Yet he had already nailed up so many new planks
that it looked as if a lot of small cupboards had been
set up round the room.

Heidi was delighted with her new home. She slept
soundly in her corner by the stove, but every morning when she first awoke she thought she was still on
the mountain. Her first impulse was to run outside
at once to see if the fir trees were so quiet because
their branches were weighed down with the thick
snow. She had to look about her for some minutes
before she felt quite sure where she was, and a certain sensation of trouble and oppression would come
over her as she realized that she was not at home in
the hut. But as soon as she heard her grandfather's
voice outside she remembered everything and jumped
happily out of bed.

On the fourth morning, as soon as she saw her
grandfather she said, "I must go up to see grandmother
today; she ought not to be alone so long."

But the grandfather would not agree to this. "Neither today nor tomorrow can you go," he said. "The
mountain is covered fathom-deep in snow, and the
snow is still falling; the sturdy Peter can hardly get
along. A little girl like you would soon be smothered

by it, and we should not be able to find you again.
Wait a bit till it freezes, then you will be able to walk
over the hard snow."

Heidi did not like the thought of having to wait,
but the days were so busy that she hardly knew how
they went by.

Heidi now went to school in Dörfli every morning
and afternoon, and eagerly set to work to learn all
that was taught her. She hardly ever saw Peter there,
for, as a rule, he was absent.

The teacher was an easygoing man, who merely
remarked now and then, "Peter is not turning up
today again, it seems, but there is a lot of snow up
on the mountain and I daresay he cannot get along."

Peter, however, always seemed able to make his
way through the snow in the evening when school
was over, for he generally paid Heidi a visit then.

One morning the whole mountain glistened and
sparkled like a huge crystal. When Peter got out of
his window as usual, he was taken by surprise, for
instead of sinking into the soft snow he fell on the
hard ground and went sliding some way down the
mountainside before he could stop himself. He
picked himself up and tested the hardness of the
ground by stamping on it and trying with all his
might to dig his heels into it, but even then he could
not break off a single little splinter of ice. The Alm

was frozen hard as iron. This was just what Peter had been hoping for.

He knew that now Heidi would be able to come up to them. He quickly got back into the house, swallowed the milk which his mother had ready for him, thrust a piece of bread in his pocket, and said, "I must be off to school."

"That's right, go and learn all you can," said the grandmother encouragingly.

The door was quite blocked by the frozen snow outside, so Peter crept through the window again, pulling his little sled after him, and in another minute was shooting down the mountain.

He went like lightning, and when he reached Dörfli, which stood on the direct road to Mayenfeld, he made up his mind to go on farther, for he was sure he could not stop his rapid descent without hurting himself and the sled too. So down he went till he reached the level ground, where the sled came to a pause of its own accord. Then he got out and looked around. The impetus with which he had made his journey down had carried him some little way beyond Mayenfeld. He thought that it was too late to get to school now, since lessons would already have begun, and it would take him a good hour to walk back to Dörfli. So he took his time about returning and reached Dörfli just as Heidi had got home from school and was sitting at dinner with her grandfather.

Peter walked in, and since on this occasion he had something particular to tell them, he began without a pause, exclaiming as he stood still in the middle of the room, "She's got it now."

"Got it? What?" asked the Uncle. "Your words sound quite warlike, general."

"The frost," explained Peter.

"Oh! Then now I can go and see grandmother!" said Heidi joyfully, for she had understood Peter's words at once. "But why were you not at school then? You could have come down on the sled," she added reproachfully, for it did not agree with Heidi's ideas of good behavior to stay away when it was possible to be there.

"It carried me on too far and I was too late," Peter replied.

"I call that being a deserter," said the Uncle, "and deserters get their ears pulled, as you know."

Peter gave a tug to his cap in alarm, for there was no one of whom he stood so much in awe as Alm-Uncle.

"And an army leader like yourself ought to be doubly ashamed of running away," continued Alm-Uncle. "What would you think of your goats if one went off this way and another that, and refused to follow and do what was good for them? What would you do then?"

"I should beat them," said Peter promptly.

"And if a boy behaved like these unruly goats, and he got a beating for it, what would you say then?"

"Serve him right," was the answer.

"Good! Then understand this: next time you let your sled carry you past the school when you ought to be inside at your lessons, come to me afterward and receive what you deserve."

Peter now understood the drift of the old man's questions and that he was the boy who behaved like the unruly goats. He looked somewhat fearfully toward the corner to see if anything happened to be there such as he used himself on such occasions for the punishment of his animals.

But now the grandfather suddenly said in a cheerful voice, "Come and sit down and have something to eat, and afterward Heidi shall go with you. Bring her back this evening and you will find supper waiting for you here."

This unexpected turn of conversation made Peter grin with delight. He obeyed without hesitation and took his seat beside Heidi. But the little girl could not eat any more in her excitement at the thought of going to see grandmother. While Peter was eating, Heidi ran to put on the warm cloak Clara had sent her.

As the two walked together Heidi had much to tell Peter. The children had nearly reached their destination before Peter opened his mouth. He appeared to be so sunk in thought that he hardly heard what was said to him. As they neared home, however, he stood still and said in a somewhat sullen voice, "I had rather go to school even than get what Uncle threatened."

Heidi was of the same mind, and encouraged him in his good intention. They found Brigitta sitting alone knitting, for the grandmother was not very well and had to stay in bed on account of the cold. Heidi had never before missed the old figure in her place in the corner, and she ran quickly into the next room. There lay grandmother on her little, poorly covered bed, wrapped up in her warm, gray shawl.

"Thank God," she exclaimed as Heidi came running in. The poor old woman had had a secret fear at heart all through the autumn, especially if Heidi was absent for any length of time. Peter had told her of a strange gentleman who had come from Frankfurt, and who had gone out with them and always talked to Heidi, and she felt sure he had come to take her away again. Even when she heard he had gone off alone, she still had an idea that a messenger would be sent over from Frankfurt to get the child.

Heidi went up to the side of the bed and said, "Are you very ill, grandmother?"

"No, no, child," answered the old woman reassuringly, passing her hand lovingly over the child's head.

"It's only the frost that has got into my bones a bit."

"Shall you be quite well then as soon as it turns warm again?"

"Yes, God willing, or even before that, for I want to get back to my spinning. I thought perhaps I should do a little today, but tomorrow I am sure to be all right again." The old woman had detected that Heidi was frightened and was anxious to set her mind at ease.

Her words comforted Heidi, who had in truth been greatly distressed, for she had never before seen the grandmother ill in bed. She now looked at the old woman seriously for a minute or two, and then said, "In Frankfurt everybody puts on a shawl to go out walking. Did you think it was to be worn in bed, grandmother?"

"I put it on, dear child, to keep myself from freezing, and I am so pleased with it, for my bedclothes are not very thick," she answered.

"But, grandmother," exclaimed Heidi, "your bed is not right, because it goes downhill at your head instead of uphill."

"I know it, child, I can feel it," and the grandmother put up her hand to the thin, flat pillow, which was little more than a board under her head. "The pillow was never very thick, and I have lain on it now for so many years that it has grown quite flat."

"Oh, if only I had asked Clara to let me take away

my Frankfurt bed!" said Heidi. "I had three large
pillows, one above the other. Could you sleep like
that, grandmother?"

"Oh, yes! The pillows keep one warm, and it is
easier to breathe when the head is high," answered
the grandmother, wearily raising her head as she spoke
as if trying to find a higher resting place. "But we
will not talk about that, for I have so much that other
old, sick people are without, for which I thank God.
There is the nice bread I get every day, and this warm
wrap, and your visits, Heidi. Will you read me
something today?"

Heidi ran into the next room to get the hymnbook.
Then she picked out the favorite hymns one after
another, for she knew now just which ones the grandmother liked best. She was as pleased as the grandmother to hear them again after so many days.

The grandmother lay with folded hands, while a
smile of peace stole over the worn, troubled face.
She looked like one to whom good news had been
brought.

Suddenly Heidi paused. "Grandmother, are you
feeling quite well again already?"

"Yes, child, I have grown better while listening to
you; read it on to the end."

The child read on, and when she came to the last
words,

" 'As the eyes grow dim, and darkness
     Closes round, the soul grows clearer,
     Sees the goal to which it travels,
     Gladly feels its home is nearer,' "

the grandmother repeated them once or twice to herself, with a look of happy expectation on her face.
And Heidi took equal pleasure in them, for the picture of the beautiful sunny day of her return home
rose before her eyes, and she exclaimed joyfully,
"Grandmother, I know exactly what it is like to go
home."

A little later Heidi said, "It is growing dark and I
must go. I am so glad to think that you are quite
well again."

The grandmother took the child's hand in hers and
held it closely. "Yes," she said, "I feel quite happy
again. Even if I have to go on lying here, I am con-
tent. No one knows what it is like to lie here alone
day after day, in silence and darkness, without hearing a new voice or seeing a ray of light. Sad thoughts
come over me, and I feel sometimes as if I could not
bear it any longer and as if it could never be light
again. But when you come and read those words to
me, then I am comforted and my heart rejoices once
more."

Then she let the child go, and Heidi ran into the
next room, and bade Peter come quickly, for it had

now grown quite dark. But when they got outside they found the moon shining down on the white snow and everything as clear as in the daylight. Peter got his sled, put Heidi at the back, he himself sitting in front to guide, and down the mountain they shot like two birds darting through the air.

When Heidi was lying that night on her high bed of hay she thought of the grandmother on her low pillow, and of all she had said about the light and comfort that awoke in her when she heard the hymns. She thought: "If I could read to her every day, then I should go on making her better." But she knew that it would be a week, if not two, before she would be able to go up the mountain again. This was a thought of great trouble to Heidi, and she tried hard to think of some way which would enable the grandmother to hear the words she loved every day. Suddenly an idea struck her, and she was so delighted with it that she could hardly bear to wait for morning, so eager was she to begin carrying out her plan.

All at once she sat upright in her bed, for she had been so busy with her thoughts that she had forgotten to say her prayers, and she never now finished her day without saying them.

When she had prayed with all her heart for herself, her grandfather, and the grandmother, she lay back again on the warm, soft hay and slept soundly and peacefully till the morning broke.

News from Distant Friends ⟨⟩

I⎯T was the month of May. The clear, warm sunshine lay upon the mountain, which had turned
green again. The last snows had disappeared, and
the sun had already coaxed many of the flowers to
show their bright heads above the grass. Up above,
the gay young wind of spring was singing through
the fir trees, and shaking down the old, dark needles
to make room for the new, bright-green ones that
were soon to deck out the trees in their spring finery.
Higher up still, the great birds went circling round
as of old, while the golden sunshine lighted up the
grandfather's hut.

Heidi was at home again on the mountain, running
back and forth in her accustomed way, not knowing
which spot was most delightful. Now she stood still
to listen to the deep, mysterious voice of the wind,
as it blew down to her from the mountain summits.
It came nearer and nearer and gathered strength as it
came, till it broke with force against the fir trees,

bending and shaking them, and seeming to shout for joy, so that she, too, though blown about like a feather, felt she must join in the chorus of exulting sounds. Then she would run around again to the sunny space in front of the hut, and seating herself on the ground would peer closely into the short grass to see how many little flower cups were open or thinking of opening.

From the shed at the back came the sound of sawing and chopping, and Heidi listened to it with pleasure, for it was the old familiar sound she had known from the beginning of her life up here. Suddenly she jumped up and ran around, for she must know what her grandfather was doing. In front of the shed door already stood a finished new chair, and a second was in course of construction under the grandfather's skilful hand.

"Oh, I know what these are for," exclaimed Heidi in great glee. "This one is for grandmamma, and the one you are now making is for Clara, and then —then there will, I suppose, have to be another," continued Heidi with more hesitation in her voice. "Or do you think, grandfather, that perhaps Miss Rottenmeier will not come with them?"

"Well, I cannot say just yet," replied her grandfather, "but it will be safer to make one so that we can offer her a seat if she does."

Heidi looked thoughtfully at the plain wooden

chair without arms as if trying to imagine how Miss Rottenmeier and a chair of this sort would suit one another. After a few minutes' contemplation, "Grandfather," she said, shaking her head doubtfully, "I don't think she would be able to sit on that."

"Then we will invite her to sit on the beautiful green couch of grass," was her grandfather's quiet rejoinder.

While Heidi was pausing to consider what this might be there sounded from above a whistling, calling, and other sounds which Heidi immediately recognized. She ran out and found herself surrounded by her four-footed friends. They were apparently as pleased as she was to be among the heights again, for they leaped about and bleated for joy, pushing Heidi this way and that, each anxious to express his delight with some sign of affection. But Peter sent them flying to right and left, for he had something to give to Heidi. When he at last got up to her he handed her a letter.

"There!" he exclaimed, leaving the further explanation of the matter to Heidi herself.

"Did someone give you this while you were out with the goats?" she asked in some surprise.

"No," answered Peter, briefly.

"Where did you get it from then?"

"I found it in the dinner bag."

That was true to a certain extent. The letter to

Heidi had been given him the evening before by the postman at Dörfli, and Peter had put it into his empty bag. That morning he had stuffed his bread and cheese on top of it, and had forgotten it, when he stopped to get Alm-Uncle's two goats. When he had finished his bread and cheese at midday and was searching in the bag for last crumbs he had found the letter which lay at the bottom.

Heidi read the address carefully. Then she ran back to the shed holding out her letter to her grandfather in high glee. "From Frankfurt! From Clara! Would you like to hear it?"

The grandfather was ready and pleased to do so, and so was Peter, who had followed Heidi into the shed.

"Dearest Heidi,—Everything is packed and we shall start now in two or three days, as soon as papa himself is ready to leave. He is not coming with us for he has to go to Paris first. The doctor comes every day, and as soon as he is inside the door, he cries, 'Off now as quickly as you can, off to the mountain.' He is most impatient about our going. You cannot think how much he enjoyed himself when he was with you! He has called nearly every day this winter, and each time he has come into my room and said he must tell me about everything again. And then he sits down and describes all he did with you and the grandfather, and talks of the mountains and the flowers and of the great silence up there far above all towns and villages, and of the fresh delicious air, and often adds, 'No one can help getting well up there.' He himself is quite a different man since his visit, and looks quite young again and happy, which he had not been for a long time before. Oh, how I am looking forward to seeing everything and to being with you on the mountain, and to making the acquaintance of Peter and the goats!

"I shall first have to go through a six weeks' cure at Ragatz, and then we shall move up to Dörfli, and every fine day I shall be carried up the mountain in my chair and spend the day with you. Grandmamma is traveling with me and will remain with me; she also is delighted at the thought of paying you a visit. But, just imagine, Miss Rottenmeier refuses to come with us. Almost every day grandmamma says to her: 'Well, how about this Swiss journey, my worthy Rottenmeier? Pray say if you really would like to come with us.' But she alwas thanks grandmamma very politely and says she has quite made up her mind. I think I know what has done it. Sebastian gave such a frightful description of the mountain, of how the rocks were so overhanging and dangerous that at any minute you might fall into a crevasse, and how it was such steep climbing that you feared at every step to go slipping to the bottom, and that goats alone could make their way up without fear of being killed. She shuddered when she heard him tell of all this, and since then she has not been so enthusiastic about Switzerland as she was before. Tinette is afraid, too, and she also refuses to come. So grandmamma and I will be alone; Sebastian will go with us as far as Ragatz and then return here.

"I can hardly wait till I see you again. Good-by, dearest Heidi; grandmamma sends you her best love and all good wishes.

—Your affectionate friend,

"CLARA."

Peter, as soon as the conclusion of the letter had been reached, rushed out, twirling his stick in the air in such a reckless fashion that the frightened goats fled down the mountain before him with higher and wider leaps than usual. Peter followed at full speed, his stick still raised in the air in a menacing manner as if he was longing to vent his fury on some invisible foe. This foe was indeed the prospect of the arrival of the Frankfurt visitors, the thought of whom filled him with exasperation.

The next afternoon Heidi ran down to tell grandmother her good news.

The grandmother sat in her corner at her spinning wheel. There was an expression on her face of mournful anxiety. Peter had come in the evening before brimful of anger and had told about the large party that was coming up from Frankfurt, and the old woman was troubled by the thought of Heidi's being taken from her.

Heidi began eagerly pouring out all her news, growing more excited with her pleasure as she went on. But all of a sudden she stopped short and said anxiously, "What is the matter, grandmother? Aren't you a bit pleased with what I am telling you?"

"Yes, yes, of course, child, since it gives you so much pleasure," the old woman answered, trying to look more cheerful.

"But I can see all the same that something troubles you. Is it because you think after all that Miss Rottenmeier may come?" asked Heidi, beginning to feel anxious herself.

"No, no! It is nothing, child," said the grandmother, wishing to reassure her. "Just give me your hand that I may feel sure you are there. No doubt

it would be the best thing for you, although I feel I
could scarcely survive it."

"I do not want anything of the best if you could
scarcely survive it," said Heidi, in a determined tone
of voice. But the grandmother was not comforted.
She felt sure the people from Frankfurt were coming
to take Heidi back with them, since she was well
again. But she was anxious to hide her trouble from
Heidi if possible.

"Heidi," she said, "there is something that would
comfort me and calm my thoughts. Read me the
hymn beginning: "All things will work for good.'"

Heidi found the place at once and read out in her
clear young voice:

> " 'All things will work for good
> To those who trust in Me;
> I come with healing on my wings,
> To save and set thee free.' "

"Yes, yes, that is just what I wanted to hear," said
the grandmother, and the deep expression of trouble
passed from her face.

When the evening came, Heidi returned home up
the mountain. The stars came out overhead one by
one, so bright and sparkling that each seemed to send
a fresh ray of joy into her heart. She was obliged
to pause continually to look up, and as the whole sky

at last grew spangled with them she spoke aloud, "Yes, I understand now why we feel so happy, and are not afraid about anything, because God knows what is good and beautiful for us." And the stars with their glistening eyes continued to nod to her till she reached home, where she found her grandfather also standing and looking up at them, for they had seldom been more glorious than they were this night.

May passed, with everything growing greener and greener, and then came the month of June, with a hotter sun and long, light days that brought the flowers out all over the mountain so that every spot was bright with them and the air full of their sweet scents. This month, too, was drawing to its close when one day Heidi, having finished her household duties, came running out of the hut. Suddenly she gave such a loud cry that her grandfather hurried out of the shed to see what had happened.

"Grandfather, grandfather" she cried, beside herself with excitement. "Come here! Look! Look!"

A strange-looking procession was making its way up the mountain. In front were two men carrying a sedan-chair, in which sat a girl well wrapped up in shawls. Then followed a horse, mounted by a stately lady who was looking about her with great interest and talking to the guide who walked beside her. Then came a rolling chair, which was being pushed by another man. Last in the procession came a porter, with such a bundle of cloaks, shawls, and furs on his back that it rose well above his head.

"Here they come! Here they come!" shouted Heidi, jumping with joy. Soon the party reached the top. The men in front put down their burden, Heidi rushed forward, and the two children embraced each other delightedly. Grandmamma dismounted and gave Heidi an affectionate greeting, before turning to the grandfather, who had meanwhile come up to welcome his guests. There was no constraint about the meeting, for they knew each other perfectly well from hearsay and felt like old acquaintances.

After the first words of greeting had been exchanged grandmamma broke out into lively expressions of admiration. "What a magnificent place you have to live in, Uncle! I could hardly have believed it was so beautiful! A king might well envy it! And how well my little Heidi looks—like a wild rose!" she continued, drawing the child toward her and stroking her fresh, pink cheeks. "I don't know which way to look first, it is all so lovely! What do you say to it, Clara, what do you say?"

Clara was gazing round entranced. She had never imagined, much less seen, anything so beautiful. She gave vent to her delight in cries of joy. "O grandmamma," she said, "I should like to remain here forever."

The grandfather had meanwhile drawn up the invalid chair and spread some of the wraps over it. He now went up to Clara.

"Suppose we carry the little daughter to her accustomed chair. I think she will be more comfortable, for the traveling sedan is rather hard," he said, and without waiting for anyone to help him he lifted the child in his strong arms and laid her gently down in her own chair. He then covered her over carefully and arranged her feet on the soft cushion, as if he had never done anything all his life but wait on cripples. The grandmamma looked on with surprise.

"My dear Uncle," she exclaimed, "if I knew where you had learned to nurse I would at once send all the nurses I know to the same place that they might handle their patients as you do."

"Uncle smiled. "I know more from experience than training," he answered.

The sky spread blue and cloudless over the hut and the fir trees and far above over the high rocks, the gray summits of which glistened in the sun. Clara could not feast her eyes enough on all the beauty around her.

"O Heidi, if only I could walk about with you," she said longingly. "If I could only go and look at the fir trees! I want to see everything you have told me about."

Heidi in response put out all her strength, and

after a slight effort, managed to wheel Clara's chair quite easily around the hut to the fir trees. There they paused. Clara had never seen such trees before, with their tall, straight stems, and long, thick branches growing thicker and thicker till they reached the ground. Even the grandmamma, who had followed the children, was astonished at the sight of them.

Heidi had now wheeled Clara on to the goat shed, and had flung open the door, so that Clara might have a full view of all that was inside. There was not much to see just now since the goats were absent. Clara lamented to her grandmother that they would have to leave early before the goats came home.

"I should so like to see Peter and his whole flock," she said regretfully.

"Dear child, let us enjoy all the beautiful things that we can see, and not think about those that we cannot," grandmamma replied as she followed the chair which Heidi was pushing farther on.

"Oh, the flowers!" exclaimed Clara. "Look at the bushes of red flowers, and all the nodding blue-bells! Oh, if I could but get out and pick some!"

Heidi ran off at once and picked her a large bunch of them.

"But these are nothing, Clara," she said, laying the flowers on her lap. "If you could come up higher to where the goats are feeding, then you would in-deed see something! Bushes on bushes of the red

centaury, and ever so many more of the blue bell-
flowers; and then the bright yellow rockroses, that
gleam like pure gold, and all crowding together in
the one spot. And then there are others with the
large leaves that grandfather calls Bright Eyes, and
the brown ones with little round heads that smell so
delicious. Oh, it is beautiful up there, and if you
sit down among them you never want to get up again,
everything looks and smells so lovely!"

Heidi's eyes sparkled with the remembrance of
what she was describing. She was longing herself to
see it all again, and Clara caught her enthusiasm and
looked back at her with equal longing in her soft,
blue eyes.

"Grandmamma, do you think I could get up there?
Is it possible for me to go?" she asked. "If only I
could walk, climb about everywhere with you, Heidi!"

"I am sure I could push you up, the chair goes so
easily," said Heidi, and in proof of her words, she
sent the chair at such a pace round the corner that
if grandmamma had not been near to stop it it might
have gone flying down the mountainside.

The grandfather, meantime, had not been idle. He
had by this time put the table and extra chairs in front
of the seat, so that they might all sit out here and eat
the dinner that was preparing inside. The milk and
the cheese were soon ready, and then the company
sat down in high spirits to their midday meal.

Grandmamma was enchanted, as the doctor had been, with their dining room, from which one could see far along the valley, and far over the mountains to the distant stretch of blue sky. A light wind blew refreshingly over them as they sat at table, and the rustling of the fir trees made a festive accompaniment to the meal.

"I never enjoyed anything as much as this. It is really superb!" cried grandmamma two or three times over. Suddenly she exclaimed in a tone of surprise, "Do I really see you taking a second piece of toasted cheese, Clara?"

There, sure enough, was a second golden-colored slice of cheese on Clara's plate.

"Oh, it does taste so good, grandmamma—better than all the dishes we have at Ragatz," replied Clara.

"That's right, eat what you can!" exclaimed Uncle. "It's the mountain air, which makes up for the deficiencies of the kitchen."

And so the meal went on. Grandmamma and Alm-Uncle got on very well together, and their conversation became more and more lively. They were so thoroughly agreed in their opinions of men and things and the world in general that they might have been taken for old cronies.

The time passed merrily, and then grandmamma looked toward the west and said, "We must soon get ready to go, Clara. The sun is a good way down.

The men will be here presently with the horse and sedan."

Clara's face fell, and she said beseechingly: "Oh, just another hour, grandmamma, or two hours. We haven't seen inside the hut yet, or Heidi's bed, or any of the other things. If only the day were ten hours long!"

"Well, that is not possible," said grandmamma, but she herself was anxious to see inside the hut, so they all rose from the table and Uncle wheeled Clara's chair to the door. There they came to a standstill, for the chair was much too broad to pass through the door. Uncle, however, soon settled the difficulty by lifting Clara in his strong arms and carrying her inside.

Grandmamma went all round and examined the household arrangements, and was very much amused and pleased at their orderliness and the cosy appearance of everything. "And this is your bedroom up here, Heidi, is it not?" she asked, as without hesitation she mounted the ladder to the hayloft. "Oh, it does smell sweet. What a healthful place to sleep in!" She went up to the round window and looked out. Grandfather followed with Clara in his arms, Heidi springing up after them. Then they all stood and examined Heidi's wonderful hay bed, and grandmamma looked thoughtfully at it and drew in from time to time fragrant drafts of the hay-perfumed air.

Clara was charmed beyond words with Heidi's sleeping apartment.

"It is delightful for you up here, Heidi! You can look from your bed straight into the sky, and there is such a delicious smell all round you. And outside the fir trees are waving and rustling. I have never seen such a pleasant, cheerful bedroom before."

Uncle looked across at grandmamma. "I have been thinking," he said to her, "that if you were willing to agree to it, your little granddaughter might remain up here, and I am sure she would grow stronger. You have brought up all kinds of shawls and covers with you, and we could make up a soft bed out of them. You need have no fear about Clara. I will be glad to look after her."

Clara and Heidi were overjoyed at these words, and grandmamma's face beamed with satisfaction.

"You are indeed kind, my dear Uncle," she exclaimed. "You give words to the thought that was in my own mind. I was only asking myself whether a stay up here might not be the very thing she wanted. But then the trouble, the inconvenience to yourself! And you speak of nursing and looking after her as if it was a mere nothing! I thank you sincerely, I thank you from my whole heart, Uncle."

Uncle carried Clara back to her chair outside and Heidi followed, not knowing how to jump high enough into the air to express her contentment.

Together Uncle and grandmamma made up a soft bed for Clara, close beside Heidi's. When the children were told that Clara was to stay for a month they clapped their hands for joy, for they had not expected to be together for so long a time.

The bearers and the horse and guide were now seen approaching, and grandmamma prepared to mount for her return journey.

"It's not saying good-by, grandmamma," Clara called out, "for you will come up now and then and see how we are getting on, and we shall so look forward to your visits, shan't we, Heidi?"

Heidi, who felt that life this day had been crowded with pleasures, could only respond to Clara with another jump of joy.

Grandmamma was now seated on her sturdy animal, and Uncle took the bridle to lead her down the steep mountain path. She begged him not to come far with her, but he insisted on seeing her safely as far as Dörfli, for the way was steep and not without danger for the rider, he said.

Grandmamma did not care to stay alone in Dörfli, and therefore decided to return to Ragatz, and from there to make excursions up the mountain from time to time.

Peter came down with his goats before Uncle had returned. As soon as the animals caught sight of Heidi they all came flocking toward her, and she and Clara on her chair were soon surrounded by the goats. They pushed and poked their heads one over the other, while Heidi introduced each in turn by its name to her friend.

Peter meanwhile stood looking on, and casting somewhat unfriendly glances toward Clara.

When the two children called out, "Good evening, Peter," he made no answer, but swung up his stick angrily, as if he wanted to cut the air in two, and then ran off with his goats after him.

The climax to all the beautiful things that Clara had already seen upon the mountain came at the close of the day.

As she lay on the large, soft bed in the hayloft, with Heidi near her, she looked out through the round, open window right into the middle of the shining clusters of stars.

"Heidi," she exclaimed in delight, "it's just as if we were in a high carriage and were going to drive straight into heaven."

"Yes, and do you know why the stars are so happy and look down and nod to us like that?" asked Heidi.

"No, why is it?" Clara asked in return.

"Because they live up in heaven, and know how well God arranges everything for us, so that we need have no more fear or trouble and may be quite sure that all things will come right in the end. That's why they are so happy, and they nod to us because they want us to be happy, too. But then we must never forget to pray, and to ask God to remember us when He is arranging things, so that we, too, may feel safe and not be afraid about what is going to happen."

The two children now sat up and said their prayers, and then Heidi put her head down on her little, round arm and fell off to sleep at once, but Clara lay awake some time. She could not get over the wonder of this new experience of being in bed up here among the stars. She had indeed seldom seen a star, for she never went outside the house at night, and the curtains at home were always drawn before the stars came out. Each time she closed her eyes she felt she must open them again to see if the two very large stars were still looking in and nodding to her as Heidi said they did. There they were, always in the same place. Clara felt she could not look long enough into their bright, sparkling faces, until at last her eyes closed of their own accord, and it was only in her dreams that she still saw the two large, friendly stars shining down upon her.

How Life Went On *&* At Grandfather's

THE sun had just risen above the mountains and was shedding its first golden rays over the hut and the valley below. Alm-Uncle, as was his custom, had been standing in a quiet and devout attitude for some little while, watching the light mists gradually lifting, and the heights and valley emerging from their twilight shadows and awakening to another day.

The light morning clouds overhead grew brighter and brighter, till at last the sun shone out in its full glory, and rock and wood and hill lay bathed in golden light.

Uncle now stepped back into the hut and went softly up the ladder. Clara had just opened her eyes and was looking with wonder at the bright sunlight that shone through the round window and danced and sparkled about her bed. She could not at first think what she was looking at or where she was. Then she caught sight of Heidi sleeping beside her, and heard the grandfather's cheery voice asking her if she had slept well and was feeling rested. She assured him she was not tired, and that when she had once fallen asleep she had not opened her eyes again all night. The grandfather was satisfied at this and immediately began to wait upon her with so much gentleness and understanding that it seemed as if his chief calling had been to look after sick children.

Heidi now awoke and was surprised to see Clara dressed, and already in the grandfather's arms ready to be carried down. She jumped up and went through her toilet with lightning-like speed. She ran down the ladder and out of the hut to where Clara was sitting in the sun.

The fresh morning breeze blew round the children's faces, and every fresh puff brought a waft of fragrance from the fir trees. Clara drew it in with delight and lay back in her chair with an unaccustomed feeling of health and comfort.

It was the first time in her life that she had been out in the open country at this early hour and felt the fresh morning breeze. The pure mountain air was so cool and refreshing that every breath she drew was a pleasure. And then the bright, sweet sun was not hot and sultry up here, but lay soft and warm on her hands and on the grass at her feet. Clara had not imagined that it would be like this on the mountain.

"O Heidi, if only I could stay up here forever with you," she exclaimed happily.

"Now you see that it is just what I told you," replied Heidi delightedly. "It is the most beautiful thing in the world to be up here with grandfather."

Uncle at that moment came from the goat shed. He brought two small, foaming bowls of snow-white milk—one for Clara and one for Heidi.

"That will do the little daughter good," he said, nodding to Clara. "It is from Little Swan and will make you strong. To your health, child! Drink it up."

Clara had never tasted goat's milk before. She hesitated and smelled it before putting it to her lips. Then, seeing how Heidi drank hers up without hesitating, and how much she seemed to like it, Clara followed her example, and drank till there was not a drop left, for she, too, found it delicious. It tasted just as if sugar and cinnamon had been mixed with it.

"Tomorrow we will drink two," said the grandfather, who had looked on with satisfaction.

Peter now arrived with the goats, and Heidi received her usual crowded morning's greeting.

When Peter marched off, the goats carried Heidi along with them a little way, which was what Peter wanted. "Aren't you coming, too?" he called to her.

"I cannot," Heidi called back from the midst of her friends, "and I shall not be able to come for a long, long time—not as long as Clara is with me. Grandfather, however, has promised to go up the mountain with both of us someday."

Heidi freed herself from the goats and ran back to Clara. As Peter went on he doubled his fists and made threatening gestures toward the invalid in her chair.

The children had promised to write to grand-mamma every day and Heidi suggested that they do that first. She ran in and brought out her schoolbook and writing things and her own little stool. She put her reading book and copybook on Clara's knees, to make a desk for her to write upon, and she herself took her seat on the stool and used the bench for a desk.

Clara paused after every sentence to look about her. The breeze had sunk a little, and now only gently fanned her face and whispered lightly through the fir trees. Little winged insects hummed and danced around her in the clear air, and a great stillness lay over the far, wide, sunny pasturelands. Lofty and silent rose the high mountain peaks above her, and below lay the whole broad valley full of quiet peace. Only now and again the call of some shepherd boy rang out through the air, and echo answered softly from the rocks.

The morning passed, the children hardly knew how, and grandfather came with the midday bowls of steaming milk. The little guest, he said, was to remain out as long as there was a gleam of sun in the sky. They spent the afternoon in the cool shade of the fir trees. Clara had much to tell Heidi about the various people who composed the Sesemann household, and who were all so well-known to Heidi.

So the hours flew by and all at once, as it seemed, the evening had come with the returning Peter, who still scowled and looked angry. He did not even answer their friendly greetings.

As Clara saw the grandfather leading away Little Swan to milk her, she was suddenly taken with a longing for another bowlful of the fragrant milk, and waited impatiently for it.

"Isn't it curious, Heidi?" she said, astonished at herself. "As long as I can remember I have eaten only because I was obliged to, and everything used to seem to taste of cod-liver oil. I was always wishing there was no need to eat or drink. And now I am longing for grandfather to bring me the milk!"

"Yes, I know what it feels like," replied Heidi, who remembered the many days in Frankfurt when all her food used to seem to stick in her throat.

When grandfather at last brought the evening milk, Clara drank hers up so quickly that she had emptied her bowl before Heidi and then she asked for a little

more. The grandfather went inside with both the
children's bowls, and when he brought them out
again full he had something else to add to their supper.
He had walked over that afternoon to a herdsman's
house where the sweet-tasting butter was made, and
had brought home a large pat, some of which he now
spread thickly on two good slices of bread. He stood
and watched with pleasure while Clara and Heidi
ate their appetizing meal with childish hunger and
enjoyment.

That night, when Clara lay down in her bed and
prepared to watch the stars, her eyes would not keep
open. She fell asleep as soon as Heidi and slept
soundly all night—a thing she never remembered having done before.

The following day and the day after passed in the
same pleasant fashion, and the third day there came
a surprise for the children. Two strong porters came
up the mountain, each carrying a bed on his shoulders with bedding of all kinds and two beautiful,
new, white coverlets. The men also had a letter
with them from grandmamma, in which she said that
the beds were for Clara and Heidi. Heidi in the
future was always to sleep in a proper bed, and when
she went down to Dörfli in the winter she was to take
one with her and leave the other at the hut, so that
Clara might always know there was a bed ready for

her when she paid a visit to the mountain. Grandmamma went on to thank the children for their long
letters and encouraged them to continue writing daily,
so that she might be able to picture all they were
doing.

The beds were set up for the children just where
they had slept before, close beside the window.

Meanwhile grandmamma down at Ragatz was re-
joicing at the excellent news of the invalid which
reached her daily from the mountain. Clara found
the life more pleasant each day. She could not say
enough of the kindness and care which the grandfather lavished upon her, nor of Heidi's lively and
amusing companionship, for her little friend was even
more entertaining than she had been in Frankfurt.
Clara's first thought when she woke each morning
was, "Oh, how glad I am to be here still!"

Since grandmamma had news each day that all
was going well with Clara, she thought she might put
off her visit to the children a little longer, for the
steep ride up and down was tiring to her.

Clara had now been on the mountain for three
weeks. For some days past the grandfather, each
morning after carrying her down, had said, "Won't
the little daughter try to stand for a minute or two?"
And Clara, to please him, had tried, but she had
clung to him as soon as her feet touched the ground,

exclaiming that it hurt her so. He let her try a little longer each day, however.

It was many years since they had had such a splendid summer among the mountains. Day after day there were the same cloudless sky and brilliant sun. The flowers opened wide their fragrant blossoms, and everywhere the eye was greeted with a glow of color. When the evening came the crimson light fell on mountain peaks and on the great snow fields, till at last the sun sank in a sea of golden flame.

Heidi never tired of telling Clara of all this, for the little visitor had never been up high enough to see the full glory of the colors. She was describing the flowers as she sat with Clara under the fir trees one evening. She had been telling her again of the wonderful light from the evening sun, when such longing came over her to see it all once more that she jumped up and ran to her grandfather, who was in the shed.

"Grandfather," she called out, almost before she was inside, "will you take us out with the goats tomorrow? Oh, it is so lovely up there now!"

"Very well," he answered, "but if I do, the little daughter must do something to please me. She must try her best again this evening to stand on her feet."

Heidi ran back with the good news to Clara. The little invalid promised to try her very best to do as the grandfather wished, for she looked forward immensely to the next day's excursion. Heidi was so pleased and excited that she called out to Peter as soon as she caught sight of him that evening.

"Peter, Peter, we are all coming out with you to-morrow and are going to stay up there the whole day."

Peter, cross as a bear, grumbled some reply, and lifted his stick to give Greenfinch a blow for no reason in particular, but Greenfinch saw the movement, and with a leap over Snowflake's back got out of the way, and the stick hit only the air.

Clara and Heidi slipped into their two fine beds that night full of their plans for the next day. They agreed to keep awake all night and talk until it was time to get up. But their heads had no sooner touched their soft pillows than the conversation suddenly ceased. Clara fell into a dream of an immense field, so thickly covered with blue bell-shaped flowers that it was the color of the sky, and Heidi heard the great bird of prey calling to her from the heights above, "Come! Come! Come!"

Something Unexpected Happens ❧

THE next day was bright and sunny. When Peter came up the mountain the grandfather was still inside with the children. Peter was a very cross-looking boy. For weeks now he had not had Heidi all to himself. When he came up in the morning the invalid child was always already in her chair and Heidi fully occupied with her. It was the same thing over again when he came down in the evening. Heidi had not come out with the goats once this summer, and now today she was bringing Clara with her, and would stick by her friend's side the whole time. It was the thought of this which was making him particularly cross this morning. There stood the chair on its high wheels. Peter seemed to see something proud and disdainful about it, and he glared at it as at an enemy that had done him harm and was likely to do him more still today. He glanced around —there was so sound anywhere, no one to see him. He sprang forward like a wild creature, caught hold of the chair and gave it a violent and angry push in the direction of the slope. The chair rolled swiftly forward and in another minute had disappeared.

Peter now sped up the mountain as if on wings, not pausing till he was well in the shelter of a large blackberry bush. He had no wish to be seen by Uncle. But he was anxious to see what had become of the chair, and his bush was well placed for that. He could watch what happened below and see what Uncle did without being discovered himself. So he looked, and there he saw his enemy running faster and faster downhill, then turning head over heels several times, and finally, after one great bound, rolling over and over to its complete destruction. The pieces flew in every direction—feet, arms, and torn fragments of the padded seat.

Peter was so delighted at the sight that he leaped in the air, laughing aloud, and stamping for joy. Now Heidi's friend would be obliged to go away, for she would have no means of going about, and when Heidi was alone again she would come out with him as in the old days, and everything would go on in the proper way again. But Peter did not consider, or did not know, that when we do a wrong thing trouble is sure to follow.

Heidi now came running out of the hut and around to the shed. Grandfather was behind with Clara in his arms. The shed stood wide open and it was quite light inside. Heidi looked into every corner and ran from one end to the other, and then stood still won-

dering what could have happened to the chair.
Grandfather now came up.

"How is this? Have you wheeled the chair away,
Heidi?"

"I have been looking everywhere for it, grandfather; you said it was standing ready outside," she
answered.

At that moment the wind, which had risen suddenly, blew open the shed door and sent it banging
back against the wall.

"It must have been the wind, grandfather," exclaimed Heidi and her eyes grew anxious at the
thought. "Oh, if it has blown the chair all the way
down to Dörfli we shall not get it back in time, and
shall not be able to go."

"If it has rolled as far as that it will never come
back, for it is in a hundred pieces by now," said the
grandfather, going round the corner and looking
down. "But it's a curious thing to have happened!"
he added as he thought over the matter. "The chair
would have had to turn a corner before starting down-
hill."

"Oh, I am sorry," lamented Clara, "for we shall
not be able to go today, or perhaps any other day.
I shall have to go home, I suppose, if I have no chair.
Oh, I am so sorry, I am so sorry!"

But Heidi looked at her grandfather with her usual
expression of confidence.

"Grandfather, you will be able to do something, won't you, so that Clara won't have to go home?" she asked.

"Well, for the present we will go up the mountain as we had arranged, and then later on we will see what can be done," he answered, much to the children's delight.

He brought out a pile of shawls, and put them in the sunniest spot he could find for Clara. Then he brought the children's morning milk and let out his two goats.

When the children had finished their breakfast the grandfather took Clara up on one arm, and the shawls on the other.

"Now then we will start," he said. "I don't know why Peter isn't here yet, but the goats can come with us."

Heidi was pleased at this and walked after her grandfather with an arm over the neck of each goat. The animals were so overjoyed to have her again that they nearly squeezed her flat between them out of sheer affection. When they reached the spot where the goats usually pastured they were surprised to find the flock already feeding there. Peter lay at full length on the ground near them.

"I'll teach you another time to go by like that, you lazy rascal! What do you mean by it?" Uncle called to him.

Peter, recognizing the voice, jumped up like a shot. "No one was up," he answered.

"Have you seen anything of the chair?" asked the grandfather.

"Of what chair?" called Peter back in answer in a surly tone of voice.

Uncle said no more. He spread the shawls on the sunny slope, and seating Clara upon them asked if she was comfortable.

"As comfortable as in my chair," she said, thanking him. "This seems the most beautiful spot. O Heidi, it is lovely, it is lovely!" she cried, looking round her with delight.

The grandfather prepared to leave them. He would come back for them toward evening. He was going now to see what had become of the chair.

The sky was dark blue, and not a single cloud was to be seen from one horizon to the other. The great snowfield above sparkled as if set with thousands and thousands of gold and silver stars. The two gray mountain peaks lifted their lofty heads against the sky and looked solemnly down upon the valley; the great bird was poised aloft in the clear, blue air, the mountain wind came over the heights and blew refreshingly around the children as they sat on the sunlit slope. It was all indescribably enjoyable to Clara and Heidi.

Some hours went by, and Heidi began to think

that she might just go over to the spot where all the flowers grew to see if they were all out and looked as lovely as the year before. Clara could not go until the grandfather came back that evening, and then the flowers probably would be already closed. The longing to go became stronger and stronger, till she felt she could not resist it.

"Would you think me unkind, Clara," she said rather hesitatingly, "if I left you for a few minutes? I should run there and back very quickly. I want to see how the flowers are looking—but wait—" An idea had come into Heidi's head. She ran and picked a bunch or two of green leaves, and then took hold of Snowflake and led her up to Clara.

"There, now you will not be alone," said Heidi, giving the goat a little push to show her she was to lie down near Clara. Heidi threw the leaves into Clara's lap and ran off. Clara began to hold out the leaves one by one to Snowflake. The goat snuggled up to her new friend in a confiding manner and slowly ate the leaves from her hand. It was easy to see that Snowflake enjoyed this peaceful and sheltered way of feeding, for when she was with the other goats she was persecuted by the larger and stronger ones of the flock.

Heidi had meanwhile reached her field of flowers, and as she caught sight of it she uttered a cry of joy. The whole ground in front of her was a mass of shimmering gold, where the rockroses spread their yellow blossoms. Above them waved whole bushes of the deep blue bell-flowers. From the whole sunlit expanse there rose a fragrance like rarest balsam. The scent came from the small brown flowers which rose modestly here and there among the yellow blossoms. Heidi stood and gazed and drew in the delicious air. Suddenly she turned and ran until she reached Clara's side, out of breath with running and excitement.

"Oh, you must come," she called out as soon as she came in sight. "It is more beautiful than you can imagine, and perhaps this evening it may not be so lovely. I believe I could carry you. Don't you think I could?"

Clara looked at her and shook her head. "Why, Heidi, what can you be thinking of! You are smaller than I am. Oh, if only I could walk!"

Heidi looked around as if in search of something. Peter was sitting up above looking down on the two children. He had been sitting and staring before him in the same way for hours, as if he could not make out what he saw. He had destroyed the chair so that Clara might not be able to move anywhere and would go home. Then a little while after that she had appeared right up here under his very nose with Heidi beside her. He thought his eyes must deceive him, and yet there she was and no mistake about it.

Heidi now looked up to where he was sitting and

called out in a firm voice, "Peter, come down here!"

"I don't wish to come," he called in reply.

"But you must! I cannot do it alone, and you must come here and help me. Make haste and come down," she commanded.

"I shall do nothing of the kind," was the answer.

Heidi ran part of the way up the slope toward him, and then pausing called again, her eyes ablaze with anger: "If you don't come at once, Peter, I will do something to you that you won't like. I mean what I say."

A great fear seized Peter when he heard that. He had done something wicked which he wanted no one to know about, and so far he had thought himself safe. But now Heidi spoke exactly as if she knew everything, and whatever she did know she would tell her grandfather. There was no one Peter feared so much as Uncle. Supposing he were to suspect what had happened about the chair! Peter's anguish of mind grew more acute. He stood up and went down to where Heidi was awaiting him.

"I am coming, and you won't do what you said."

Peter appeared now so submissive with fear that Heidi felt quite sorry for him and answered assuringly, "No, no, of course not. Come along with me, there is nothing to be afraid of."

As soon as they got to Clara, Heidi gave her orders. Peter was to take hold of her under the arm on one side and she on the other, and together they were to lift her up. This first movement was successfully carried through, but then came the difficulty. Since Clara could not even stand, how were they to support her and get her along? Heidi was too small for her arm to serve Clara to lean upon.

"You must put one arm well round my neck—so, and put the other through Peter's and lean firmly upon it. Then we shall be able to carry you."

Peter, however, had never given his arm to anyone in his life. Clara put hers in his, but he kept his own hanging down straight beside him like a stick.

"That's not the way, Peter," said Heidi in an authoritative voice. "You must put your arm out in the shape of a ring, and Clara must put hers through it and lean her weight upon you. Whatever you do, don't let your arm give way! Like that I am sure we shall be able to manage."

Peter did as he was told, but still they did not get on very well. Clara was not a lightweight, and the team did not match very well in size. It was up one side and down the other, so that the supports were rather wobbly.

Clara tried to use her own feet a little, but each time drew them quickly back.

"Put your foot down firmly once," suggested Heidi. "I am sure it will hurt you less after that."

"Do you think so?" said Clara hesitatingly, but she followed Heidi's advice and ventured one firm step on the ground and then another. She cried out a little as she did it, but she lifted her foot again and went on. "Oh, that was less painful already!" she exclaimed joyfully.

"Try again," said Heidi encouragingly.

And Clara went on putting one foot down after the other until all at once she called out: "I can do it, Heidi! Look! Look! I can make proper steps!"

And Heidi cried out with even greater delight, "Can you really make steps, can you really walk? Really walk by yourself? Oh, if only grandfather were here!" She continued gleefully to exclaim, "You can walk now, Clara, you can walk!"

Clara still held on firmly to her supports, but with

every step she felt safer on her feet, and Heidi was beside herself with joy.

"Now we shall be able to come up here together every day, and go just where we like. You will be able all your life to walk about as I do, and not have to be pushed in a chair, and you will get quite strong and well. It is the greatest happiness we could have had!"

And Clara heartily agreed, for she could think of no greater joy in the world than to be strong and able to go about like other people, and no longer to have to lie from day to day in her invalid chair.

They had not far to go to reach the field of flowers, and could already catch sight of the rockroses glowing gold in the sun. When they came to the bushes of the blue bellflowers, with sunny, inviting patches of warm ground between them, they sat down in the midst of the flowers. It was the first time Clara had sat on the dry, warm mountain grass, and she found it indescribably delightful. Around them were the blue flowers softly waving to and fro, and beyond the gleaming patches of the yellow rockroses and the red centaury, while the sweet scent of the brown blossoms and of the fragrant prunella enveloped them. Clara sat silent, overcome with the enchantment of all that her eye rested upon, and with the anticipation of all the happiness that was now before her.

Peter lay among the flowers without moving or

speaking, for he was fast asleep. The breeze came blowing softly and caressingly from behind the sheltering rocks, and passed whisperingly through the bushes overhead.

It was long past noon when a small troop of goats advanced solemnly toward the plain of flowers. It was not a feeding place of theirs, for they did not care to graze on flowers. They looked like an embassy arriving, with Greenfinch as their leader. They had evidently come in search of their companions who had left them in the lurch, and who had, contrary to all custom, remained away so long, for the goats could tell the time without mistake. As soon as Greenfinch caught sight of the three missing friends amid the flowers she set up an extra loud bleat, whereupon all the others joined in a chorus of bleats, and the whole company came trotting toward the children.

Peter woke up, rubbing his eyes, for he had been dreaming that he saw the chair again with its beautiful red padding standing whole and uninjured before the grandfather's door. Just as he awoke he thought he was looking at the brass-headed nails that studded it all around, but it was only the bright, yellow flowers beside him. He experienced again the dreadful fear of mind that he had lost in this dream of the uninjured chair. Even though Heidi had promised not to do anything, there still remained the lively dread that his deed might be found out in some other way.

When all three had got back to their former place Heidi ran and brought forward the bag, and proceeded to keep her promise, for her threat of the morning had been concerned with Peter's dinner. She had seen her grandfather putting in all sorts of good things, and had been pleased to think of Peter's having a large share of them. She had meant him to understand when he refused at first to help her that he would get nothing for his dinner, but Peter's conscience had put another interpretation upon her words. Heidi took the food out of the bag and divided it into three portions, and each was of such a goodly size that she thought to herself, "There will be plenty of ours left for him to have more still."

She gave the other two their dinners and sat down with her own beside Clara, and they all three ate with a good appetite after their great exertions.

They were so late at their dinner that they had not long to wait after they had finished before grandfather came up for them. Heidi rushed forward to meet him as soon as he appeared, for she wanted to be the first to tell him the good news. She was so excited that she could hardly get her words out, but he soon understood, and a look of extreme pleasure came into his face. He hastened up to where Clara was sitting and said with a cheerful smile, "So we've made the effort, have we, and won the day!"

Then he lifted her up, and putting his left arm around her and giving her his right to lean upon, made her walk a little way.

Heidi skipped along beside her in triumphant glee, and the grandfather, too, looked very happy. But soon he took Clara up in his arms. "We must not overdo it," he said, "and it is high time we went home." He hurried down the mountain path, for he was anxious to get Clara indoors so that she might rest after her unusual fatigue.

When Peter got to Dörfli that evening he found a large group of people collected around a certain spot, pushing one another and looking over one another's shoulders in their eagerness to catch sight of something lying on the ground. Peter thought he should like to see too, and poked and elbowed till he made his way through.

Scattered about the grass were the remains of Clara's chair, part of the back and the middle bit, and enough of the red padding and the bright nails to show how magnificent the chair had been when it was entire.

"I was here when the men passed carrying it up," said the baker, who was standing near Peter. "I'll bet anyone that it was worth one hundred twenty dollars at least. I cannot think how such an accident could have happened."

"Uncle said the wind might perhaps have done it," remarked one of the women, who could not sufficiently admire the red upholstery.

"It's a good job that no one but the wind did it," said the baker again, "or he might smart for it! No doubt the gentleman in Frankfurt when he hears what has happened will make all inquiries about it. I am glad for myself that I have not been seen up the mountain for a good two years, for suspicion is likely to fall on anyone who was up there at the time."

Many more opinions were passed on the matter, but Peter had heard enough. He crept quietly away out of the crowd and then took to his heels and ran up home as fast as he could, as if he thought someone was after him. The baker's words had filled him with fear. He was sure now that any day a constable might come over from Frankfurt and inquire about the destruction of the chair, and then everything would come out, and he would be seized and carried off to Frankfurt and there put in prison. His hair stood on end with terror.

He reached home in this disturbed state of mind. He would not open his mouth in reply to anything that was said to him. He would not eat his potatoes. All he did was to creep off to bed as quickly as possible and hide under the bedclothes and groan.

"Peter has been eating sorrel again, and is evidently in pain by the way he is groaning," said Brigitta.

"You must give him a little more bread to take with him; give him a bit of mine tomorrow," said the grandmother sympathizingly.

As the little girls lay that night in bed looking out at the stars Heidi said, "I have been thinking all day what a happy thing it is that God does not give us what we ask for, even when we pray and pray and pray, if He knows there is something better for us. Have you felt like that?"

"Why do you ask me that tonight all of a sudden?" asked Clara.

"Because I prayed so hard when I was in Frankfurt that I might go home at once, and when I was not allowed to I thought God had forgotten me. And now you see, if I had come away at first when I wanted to, you would never have come here, and would never have got well."

Clara had in her turn become thoughtful. "But, Heidi," she said, "in that case we ought never to pray for anything, for God always intends something better for us than we know or wish for."

"You must not think it is like that, Clara," replied Heidi eagerly. "We must go on praying for everything, so that God may know we do not forget that it all comes from Him. If we forget God, then He lets us go our own way and we get into trouble; grandmamma told me so. And if He does not give us what we ask for we must not think that He has

not heard us and stop praying, but we must still pray
and say, 'I am sure, dear God, that Thou art keeping
something better for me, and I will not be unhappy,
for I know that Thou wilt make everything right in
the end.' "

"How did you learn all that?" asked Clara.

"Grandmamma explained it to me first of all, and
then when it all happened just as she said, I knew it
myself, and I think, Clara," she went on, as she sat
up in bed, "we ought certainly to thank God tonight
that you can walk now, and that He has made us so
happy."

"Yes, Heidi, I am sure you are right, and I am glad
you reminded me. I almost forgot my prayers for
very joy."

Both children said their prayers, and each thanked
God in her own way for the blessing He had be-
stowed on Clara, who had for so long lain weak and
ill.

The next morning the grandfather suggested that
they should now write to the grandmamma and ask
her if she would not come and pay them a visit, since
they had something new to show her. But the children had another plan in their heads, for they wanted
to prepare a great surprise for grandmamma. Clara
was first to have more practice in walking so that
she might be able to go a little way by herself. Above
all things grandmamma was not to have a hint of it.

They asked the grandfather how long he thought this would take, and when he told them about a week or less, they immediately sat down and wrote a pressing invitation to grandmamma, asking her to come soon, but no word was said about there being anything new to see.

The following days were some of the most joyous that Clara had spent on the mountain. She awoke each morning with a happy voice within her crying, "I am well now! I am well now! I shan't have to go about in a chair, I can walk by myself like other people."

Then came the walking, and every day she found it easier and was able to go a longer distance. The exercise gave her such an appetite that the grandfather cut his bread and butter a little thicker each day, and was well pleased to see it disappear. He now brought out with it a large jugful of the foaming milk and filled her little bowl over and over again. And so another week went by and the day came which was to bring grandmamma up the mountain for her second visit.

"Good-By till We Meet Again" ⟳

GRANDFATHER and the children were already outside with the goats when Peter came up with his flock one morning. He brought with him a letter from grandmamma. As he neared the group his steps slackened. The instant he had handed the letter to Uncle he turned quickly away as if frightened, and as he went he gave a hasty glance behind him, and then with a leap he ran off up the mountain.

"Grandfather," said Heidi, who had been watching him with astonished eyes, "why does Peter always behave now like the Great Turk when he thinks somebody is after him with a stick?"

"Perhaps Peter fancies he sees the stick which he so well deserves coming after him," answered grandfather.

When Peter was well out of sight he stood still and looked suspiciously about him. Suddenly he gave a jump and looked behind him with a terrified expression, for he expected every minute that the police

252

constable from Frankfurt would leap out upon him from behind some bush or hedge.

Mrs. Sesemann had written to say she would be up that very day. Heidi immediately set about straightening up the hut, for grandmamma must find everything clean and in good order when she arrived.

So the morning soon went by, and grandmamma might now be expected at any minute. The children dressed themselves and went and sat outside on the seat ready to receive her.

Grandfather came to show them the splendid bunch of blue gentians which he had been up the mountain to gather, and the children exclaimed with delight at the beauty of the flowers as they shone in the morning sun.

Heidi jumped up from time to time to see if there was any sign of grandmamma's approach. At last she saw the procession winding up the mountain just in the order she had expected. First there was the guide, then the white horse with grandmamma mounted upon it, and last of all the porter with a heavy bundle on his back, for grandmamma would not think of going up the mountain without a full supply of wraps and rugs.

Nearer and nearer wound the procession. At last it reached the top and grandmamma was there looking down on the children from her horse. She no sooner saw them, however, sitting side by side, than she began quickly dismounting, as she cried out in a shocked tone of voice, "Why is this? Why are you not lying in your chair, Clara? What are you all thinking about?" But even before she had got close to them she threw up her hands in astonishment, exclaiming further, "Is it really you, dear child? Why, your cheeks have grown quite round and rosy! I should hardly have known you!"

She was hastening forward to embrace her granddaughter, when the two children slipped down from the seat and began walking toward her quite coolly and naturally. Laughing and crying, grandmamma ran to them and embraced first Clara and then Heidi, and then Clara again, unable to speak for joy. All at once she caught sight of Uncle looking on smilingly at the meeting. She took Clara's arm in hers, overjoyed at the fact that the child could now really walk about with her and went up to the old man. Letting go Clara's arm she seized his hands.

"My dear Uncle! My dear Uncle! How much we have to thank you for! It is all your doing! It is your care and nursing—"

"And God's good sun and mountain air," he interrupted her, smiling.

"Yes, and don't forget the beautiful milk I have," put in Clara. "Grandmamma, you can't think what a quantity of goat's milk I drink, and how good it is!"

"I can see that by your cheeks, child," answered

grandmamma. "I really should not have known you. You have grown quite strong and plump, and taller, too. I never hoped or expected to see you look like that. I cannot take my eyes off you, for I can hardly yet believe it. But now I must telegraph without delay to your father in Paris, and tell him he must come here at once. It will be the greatest happiness he has ever known! My dear Uncle, how can I send a telegram? Have you dismissed the men yet?"

"They have gone," he answered, "but if you are in a hurry I will call Peter, and he can take it for you."

Uncle went aside a little way and blew such a resounding whistle through his fingers that he woke a responsive echo among the rocks far overhead. He did not have to wait many minutes before Peter came running down, looking as white as a ghost, for he quite thought Uncle was sending for him to give him up. But Uncle simply gave him a paper with instructions to take it down at once to the post office at Dörfli.

Peter went off with the paper in his hand, feeling some relief of mind for the present.

Meanwhile Mr. Sesemann, who had finished his business in Paris, had also been preparing a surprise. Without writing to his mother he got into the train one sunny morning and traveled that day to Basle. The next morning he continued his journey, for a great longing had seized him to see his little daughter

from whom he had been separated the whole summer.
He arrived at Ragatz a few hours after his mother
had left. When he heard that she had that very day
started for the mountain, he immediately hired a carriage and drove to Dörfli.

The climb up the mountain from Dörfli proved
long and fatiguing to Mr. Sesemann. He went on
and on, but still no hut came in sight, and yet he knew
there was one where Peter lived, halfway up, for the
path had been described to him over and over again.

There were traces of climbers to be seen on all
sides. The narrow footpaths seemed to run in every
direction, and Mr. Sesemann began to wonder if he
was on the right one, and whether the hut lay perhaps on the other side of the mountain. He looked
around to see if there was anyone in sight of whom
he could ask the way, but there was not a soul to be
seen.

Mr. Sesemann stood still for a while to let the cool
Alpine wind blow on his hot face. Soon someone
came running down the mountainside. It was Peter
with the telegram in his hand. He ran straight down
the steep slope, not following the path on which Mr.
Sesemann was standing. As soon as the gentleman
caught sight of him he beckoned to him. Peter advanced toward him slowly and timidly, with a sort
of sidelong movement, as if he could move only one
leg properly and had to drag the other after him.

"Hurry up, lad," called Mr. Sesemann, and when Peter was near enough, "Tell me," he said, "is this the way to the hut where the old man and the child Heidi live, and where the visitors from Frankfurt are staying?"

A low sound of fear was the only answer he received, and Peter turned and ran in such haste that he fell head over heels several times, and went rolling and bumping down the slope, just as the chair had done, but Peter fortunately did not fall to pieces. Only the telegram came to grief, and that was torn into fragments and blown away.

"How extraordinarily timid these mountain dwellers are!" thought Mr. Sesemann to himself.

After watching Peter's violent descent toward the valley for a few minutes he continued his journey.

Peter, meanwhile, with all his efforts, could not stop himself, but went rolling on, and still tumbling head over heels at intervals in a most remarkable manner.

But this was not the most terrible part of his sufferings at the moment, for far worse was the fear and horror that possessed him. He felt sure that the policeman had really come over for him from Frankfurt. He had no doubt at all that the stranger who had asked him the way was the very man himself. Just as he had rolled to the edge of the last high slope above Dörfli he was caught in a bush, and at last able to keep himself from falling any farther. He lay still for a second or two to recover himself, and to think over matters.

"Well done!" said a voice close to Peter. "And which of you is the wind going to send rolling down tomorrow like a sack of potatoes?" It was the baker, who stood there, laughing. He had been strolling out to refresh himself after his hot day's work, and had watched with amusement as he saw Peter come rolling over and over in much the same way as the chair.

Peter was on his feet in a moment. He had received a fresh shock. Without once looking behind him he began hurrying up the slope again. He would have liked best to go home and creep into bed, to hide himself, for he felt safest there. But he had left the goats up above, and Uncle had given him strict orders to hurry back so that they might not be left too long alone. There was no help for it, he had to go back, and Peter went on groaning and limping. He could run no more, for the anguish of mind he had been through, and the bumping and shaking he had received, were beginning to tell upon him.

Shortly after he had met Peter, Mr. Sesemann passed the first hut, and so was satisfied that he was on the right path. He continued his climb with renewed courage, and at last, after a long and exhaust-

ing walk, he came in sight of his goal. There, only a little distance farther up, stood the grandfather's home, with the dark tops of the fir trees waving above its roof.

Mr. Sesemann was delighted to have come to the last steep bit of his journey. In another minute or two he would be with his little daughter, and he was happy at the thought of her surprise. But the company above had seen him approaching and had recognized him, and they were preparing something he little expected as a surprise on their part.

As he stepped up on the space in front of the hut

two girls came toward him. One was tall, with fair hair and pink cheeks. She leaned on Heidi, whose dark eyes were dancing with joy. Mr. Sesemann suddenly stopped, staring at the two children, and all at once the tears started to his eyes. What memories arose in his heart! Just so had Clara's mother looked, with her fair hair and delicate pink-and-white complexion. Mr. Sesemann did not know whether he was awake or dreaming.

"Don't you know me, papa?" called Clara to him, her face beaming with happiness. "Am I so changed since you saw me?"

Then Mr. Sesemann ran to his child and clasped her in her arms.

"Yes, you are indeed changed! How is it possible? Is what I see true?" And the delighted father stepped back to look at her again, and to make sure that the picture would not vanish before his eyes.

"Are you my little Clara, really my little Clara?" he kept on saying, as he clasped her in his arms again, and again put her away from him that he might look and make sure it was she who stood before him.

And now grandmamma came up, anxious for a sight of her son's happy face.

"Well, what do you say now, dear son?" she exclaimed. "You have given us a pleasant surprise, but it is nothing in comparison to what we have prepared

for you, you must confess." She gave her son an
affectionate kiss as she spoke. "But now," she went
on, "you must come and pay your respects to Uncle,
who is our chief benefactor."

"Yes, indeed, and to the little inmate of our own
house, our little Heidi, too," said Mr. Sesemann, shaking Heidi by the hand. "Well? Are you still well
and happy in your mountain home? But I need not
ask. No Alpine rose could look more blooming. I
am glad, child. It is a pleasure to me to see you so."

And Heidi looked up with equal pleasure into
Mr. Sesemann's kind face. How good he had always
been to her! And that he should find such happiness
awaiting him on the mountain made her heart beat
fast with gladness.

Grandmamma now introduced her son to Uncle.
While the two men were shaking hands and Mr. Sesemann was expressing his heartfelt thanks and boundless
astonishment to the old man, grandmamma wandered
round to the back to see the old fir trees again.

Here another unexpected sight met her gaze, for
there, under the trees where the long branches had
left a clear space on the ground, stood a great clump of
the most wonderful dark-blue gentians, as fresh and
shining as if they were growing on the spot. She
clasped her hands, enraptured with their beauty.

"How exquisite! What a lovely sight!" she exclaimed. "Heidi, dearest child, come here! Is it you who have prepared this pleasure for me? It is perfectly wonderful!"

The children ran up.

"No, no, I did not put them there," said Heidi, "but I know who did."

"They grow just like that on the mountain, grandmamma, only if anything they look more beautiful still," Clara put in. "But guess who brought those down today."

At this moment a slight rustling was heard behind the fir trees. It was Peter, who had just arrived. He had seen from a distance who it was standing beside Uncle in front of the hut, and he was trying to slip by unobserved. But grandmamma had seen and recognized him, and suddenly the thought struck her that it might be Peter who had brought the flowers and that he was now trying to get away unseen, feeling shy about it.

"Come along, my boy. Come here, do not be afraid," she called to him.

Peter stood still, petrified with fear. After all he had gone through that day he felt he had no longer any power of resistance left. All he could think was, "It's all up with me now." Every hair of his head stood on end, and he stepped forth from behind the fir trees, his face pale and distorted with terror.

"Don't be afraid, my boy," said grandmamma in

an effort to put him at his ease. "Tell me now straight out, was it you who did it?"

Peter did not lift his eyes and therefore did not see at what grandmamma was pointing. But he knew that Uncle was standing at the corner of the hut, fixing him with his gray eyes, while beside him stood the most terrible person that Peter could think of—the police constable from Frankfurt. Quaking in every limb, and with trembling lips the lad muttered a low "Yes."

"Well, and what is there dreadful about that?" said grandmamma.

"Because—because—it is all broken to pieces and no one can put it together again." Peter brought out his words with difficulty, and his knees knocked together so that he could hardly stand.

Grandmamma went up to Uncle. "Is that poor boy a little out of his mind?" she asked sympathizingly.

"Not in the least," Uncle assured her. "It is only that he was the wind that sent the chair rolling down the slope, and he is expecting his well-deserved punishment."

Uncle was simply giving expression to the suspicion that he had had from the moment the accident happened. The angry looks which Peter had from the beginning cast at Clara, and the other signs of his dislike for what had been taking place on the mountain, had not escaped Uncle's eye. Putting two and two together he had come to the right conclusion as to the cause of the disaster, and he therefore spoke without hesitation when he accused Peter.

"No, no, dear Uncle," grandmamma protested, "we will not punish the poor boy any further. We must be fair to him. Here are all these strangers from Frankfurt who come and carry away Heidi, his one possession, and a possession well worth having too, and he is left to sit alone day after day for weeks, with nothing to do but brood over his wrongs. No, no, let us be fair to him. His anger got the upper hand and drove him to an act of revenge—a foolish one, I own, but then we all behave foolishly when we are angry." And saying this she went back to Peter, who still stood frightened and trembling. She sat down on the seat under the fir trees and called him to her kindly.

"Come here, my boy, and stand in front of me, for I have something to say to you. Stop shaking and trembling, for I want you to listen to me. You sent the chair rolling down the mountain so that it was broken to pieces. That was a very wrong thing to do, as you yourself knew very well at the time. You also knew that you deserved to be punished for it, and in order to escape this you have been doing all you can to hide the truth from everybody. But be sure of this, Peter. Those who do wrong make a mistake when they think no one knows anything about it. For

God sees and hears everything, and when the wicked doer tries to hide what he has done, then God wakes up the little watchman that He places inside us all when we are born and who sleeps on quietly till we do something wrong. And the little watchman has a small goad in his hand, and when he wakes up he keeps on pricking us with it, so that we have not a moment's peace. And the watchman torments us still further, for he keeps on calling out, 'Now you will be found out. Now they will drag you off to punishment!' And so we pass our life in fear and trouble, and never know a moment's happiness or peace. Have you not felt something like that lately, Peter?"

Peter gave a contrite nod of the head, for grandmamma had described his own feelings exactly.

"And you calculated wrongly also in another way," continued grandmamma, "for you see the harm you intended has turned out for the best for those you wished to hurt. Since Clara had no chair to go in and yet wanted so much to see the flowers, she made the effort to walk, and everyday since she has been walking better and better. If she remains up here she will in time be able to go up the mountain every day, much oftener than she would have done in her chair. So you see, Peter, God brought good out of evil for those whom you meant to injure, and you who did the evil were left to suffer the unhappy consequences of it. Do you thoroughly understand all I have said to you,

Peter? If so, do not forget my words, and whenever
you feel inclined to do anything wrong, think of the
little watchman inside you with his goad and his dis-
agreeable voice. Will you remember all this?"

"Yes, I will," answered Peter, still very subdued.
He did not yet know how the matter was going to
end, for the police constable was still standing with
the Uncle.

"That's right, and now the thing is over and done
for," said grandmamma. "But I should like you to
have something for a pleasant reminder of the visitors
from Frankfurt. Can you tell me anything that you
have wished very much to have? What would you
like best as a present?"

Peter lifted his head at this, and stared open-eyed
at grandmamma. Up to the last minute he had been
expecting something dreadful to happen, and now,
instead, he might have anything that he wanted. His
mind seemed all in a whirl.

"I mean what I say," grandmamma assured him.
"You shall choose what you would like to have as a
remembrance from the Frankfurt visitors, and as a
token that they will not think any more of the wrong
thing you did. Now do you understand me, boy?"

The fact began at last to dawn upon Peter's mind
that he had no further punishment to fear, and that
the kind lady sitting in front of him had delivered him
from the police constable. He suddenly felt as if the

weight of a mountain had fallen off him. He had also by this time awakened to the further conviction that it was better to make a full confession at once of anything he had done wrong or had left undone, and so he said, "And I lost the paper, too."

Grandmamma had to consider a moment what he meant, but soon recalled his connection with her telegram.

"You are a good boy to tell me!" she said kindly. "Never conceal anything you have done wrong, and then all will come right again. And now what would you like me to give you?"

Peter grew almost giddy with the thought that he could have anything in the world that he wished for. He had a vision of the yearly fair at Mayenfeld with the glittering stalls and all the lovely things that he had stood gazing at for hours, without a hope of ever possessing one of them. Peter's purse never held more than a cent, and all these fascinating objects cost more than double that amount.

Peter stood lost in thought. He was trying to think whether he would rather have a red whistle or a knife. Then a bright thought occurred to him. If he had the money he would be able to think over the matter between now and next year's fair.

"A nickel," he answered, no longer in doubt.

Grandmamma could not help laughing. "That is not an extravagant request. Come here, then!" and she pulled out her purse and put five bright, round half dollars in his hand and then laid a dime on the top. "We will settle our accounts at once," she said, "and I will explain them to you. I have given you as many nickels as there are weeks in the year, and so every Monday throughout the year you can have a nickel to spend."

"As long as I live?" Asked Peter quite innocently.

Grandmamma laughed still more at this, and the men, hearing her, paused in their talk to listen to what was going on.

"Yes, my boy, you shall have it all your life—I will put it down in my will. Do you hear, my son? You are to put it down in yours as well: a nickel a week to Peter as long as he lives."

Mr. Sesemann nodded his assent and joined in the laughter.

Peter looked again at the present in his hand to make sure he was not dreaming, and then said, "Thank God!"

And he went off running and leaping with even more than his usual agility, and this time managed to keep his feet, for it was not fear, but joy such as he had never known before in his life, that now sent him flying up the mountain. All trouble had disappeared, and he was to have a nickel every week for life.

After dinner, when the party were sitting together chatting, Clara drew her father a little aside, and said with an eagerness that had been unknown to the little tired invalid: "O papa, if you only knew all that grandfather has done for me from day to day! I cannot count his kindnesses, but I shall never forget them as long as I live! And I keep on wondering what I could do for him that would give him half as much pleasure as he has given me."

"That is just what I want to do myself, Clara," replied her father, whose face grew happier each time he looked at his little daughter. "I have also been wondering how we can best show our gratitude to our good benefactor."

Mr. Sesemann now went over to where Uncle and grandmamma were engaged in lively conversation.

Taking Uncle by the hand he said: "Dear friend, you will believe me when I tell you that I have known no real happiness for years past. What were money and property worth to me when they could not make my poor child well and happy? With the help of God you have made her whole and strong, and you have given new life not only to her but to me. Tell me now, in what way can I show my gratitude to you? I can never repay all you have done, but whatever is in my power to do is at your service. Speak, friend, and tell me what I can do."

Uncle had listened to him quietly, with a smile of pleasure on his face as he looked at the happy father.

"Mr. Sesemann," he replied in his dignified way,

"believe me that I too have my share in the joy of your daughter's recovery, and my trouble is well repaid by it. I thank you heartily for all you have said, but I have need of nothing. I have enough for myself and the child as long as I live. One wish alone I have, and if that could be satisfied I should have no further care in life."

"Speak, dear friend, and tell me what it is," begged Mr. Sesemann.

"I am growing old," Uncle said, "and shall not be here much longer. I have nothing to leave the child when I die, and she has no relatives, except one person who will always like to make what profit out of her she can. If you could promise me that Heidi would never have to go and earn her living among strangers, then you would richly reward me for all I have done for your child."

"There could never be any question of such a thing as that, my dear friend," said Mr. Sesemann quickly. "I look upon the child as our own. Ask my mother, my daughter; you may be sure that they will never allow the child to be left in anyone else's care! But if it will make you happier I give you my hand upon it. I promise you: Heidi shall never have to go and earn her living among strangers; I will make provision against this both during my life and after. But now I have something else to say. The child is totally unfitted to live a life away from home. We found that out when she was with us. But she has made friends, and among them I know one who is at this moment in Frankfurt. He is winding up his affairs there, that he may be free to go where he likes and take his rest. I am speaking of my friend, the doctor, who came over here in the autumn and who intends to settle in this neighborhood. So you see the child will from now on have two protectors near her —and may both live long to share the task!"

"God grant indeed it may be so!" added grandmamma, shaking Uncle's hand warmly as she spoke. Then putting her arm around Heidi she drew the child to her.

"And I have a question to ask you too, dear Heidi. Tell me if there is anything you particularly wish for."

"Yes, there is," answered Heidi promptly, looking up delightedly at grandmamma.

"Then tell me at once, dear, what it is."

"I want to have the bed I slept in at Frankfurt with the high pillows and the thick coverlet, and then Grandmother will not have to lie with her head down-hill, hardly able to breathe, and she will be warm enough under the coverlet not to have to wear her shawl in bed to prevent her freezing to death."

In her eagerness to obtain what she had set her heart

upon Heidi hardly gave herself time to get out all
she had to say, and did not pause for breath till she
reached the end of her sentence.

"Dearest child," answered grandmamma, moved
by Heidi's speech, "what is this you tell me of grandmother! You are right to remind me. In the midst of
our own happiness we forget too often that which
we ought to remember before all things. When God
has shown us some special mercy we should think at
once of those who are denied so many things. I will
telegraph to Frankfurt at once! Miss Rottenmeier
shall pack up the bed this very day, and it will be here
in two days' time. God willing, grandmother shall
soon be sleeping comfortably upon it."

Heidi skipped around grandmamma in her glee,
and then stopping all of a sudden she said quickly,
"I must hurry down and tell grandmother!"

They all decided to go down to see the grandmother, but before they started Mr. Sesemann told
them his plans. He had been arranging that he and
his mother should make a little tour in Switzerland,
taking Clara with them as far as she was able to go.
But now that he could take his little daughter all the
way, he wanted to start at once. And so he proposed
that he and his mother should spend the night in
Dörfli and that the next day he should come and get
Clara. Then they would all three go down to Ragatz
and make that their starting point.

Clara was rather upset at first at the thought of saying good-by like this to her friends on the mountain. She could not help being pleased, however, at the prospect of the journey.

Grandmamma took Heidi by the hand, and they led the way down the mountain. Uncle came next with Clara in his arms, for she could not yet walk that far. Mr. Sesemann brought up the rear.

Brigitta saw the company approaching and rushed indoors.

"The whole party of them are just going past, mother, evidently all returning home again," she informed the old woman. "Uncle is with them, carrying the sick child."

"Alas, is it really to be so then?" sighed the grandmother. "And you saw Heidi with them? Then they are taking her away. If only she could come and put her hand in mine again! If I could but hear her voice once more!"

At this moment the door flew open and Heidi sprang across to the corner and threw her arms around grandmother.

"Grandmother! Grandmother! My bed is to be sent from Frankfurt with all the three pillows and the thick coverlet. Grandmamma says it will be here in two days." Heidi could not get out her words quickly enough, for she was impatient to see grandmother's joy at the news.

The old woman smiled, but she said a little sadly, "She must indeed be a good, kind lady, and I ought to be glad to think she is taking you with her, but I shall not outlive it long."

"What is this I hear? Who has been telling my good grandmother such tales?" exclaimed a kindly voice, and grandmother felt her hand taken and warmly pressed. Grandmamma had followed Heidi in and heard all that was said. "No, no, there is no thought of such a thing! Heidi is going to stay with you and make you happy. We want to see her again, but we shall come to her. We hope to pay a visit to the Alm every year, for we have good cause to offer up especial thanks to God upon this spot where so great a miracle has been wrought upon our child."

And now grandmother's face was lighted up with geniune happiness, and she pressed Mrs. Sesemann's hand over and over again, unable to speak her thanks, while two large tears of joy rolled down her aged cheeks.

"How many, many other good things God has sent me," said the grandmother, deeply moved. "I did not think it possible that there were so many kind people, ready to trouble themselves about a poor old woman and to do so much for her. Nothing strengthens our belief in a kind heavenly Father who never forgets even the least of His creatures so much as to know that there are such people, full of goodness and pity for a poor, useless creature such as I am."

"My good grandmother," said Mrs. Sesemann, interrupting her, "we are all equally poor and helpless in the eyes of God, and we all have equal need that He should not forget us. But now we must say good-by, but only till we meet again, for when we pay our next year's visit to the Alm you will be the first person we shall come and see. Meanwhile we shall not forget you." And Mrs. Sesemann took grandmother's hand again in farewell.

Mr. Sesemann and his mother continued their journey down, while Uncle carried Clara back home, Heidi ran along beside him, so full of joy of what was coming for grandmother that every step was a jump.

But there were many tears shed the following morning by the departing Clara, who wept to say good-by to her friends and the beautiful mountain home where she had been happier than ever in her life before. Heidi did her best to comfort her.

"Summer will be here again in no time," she said, "and then you will come again, and it will be nicer still, for you will be able to walk about from the beginning. We can go out every day with the goats up to where the flowers grow, and enjoy ourselves from the moment you arrive."

Mr. Sesemann arrived to take his little daughter away, and Clara, somewhat consoled by Heidi's words, turned to her little friend.

"Be sure you say good-by for me to Peter and the goats, and especially to Little Swan. I wish I could give Little Swan a present, for she has helped so much to make me strong."

"Well, you can if you like," replied Heidi. "Send her a little salt. You know how she likes to lick some out of grandfather's hand when she comes home at night."

Clara was delighted at this idea. "Oh, then I shall send a hundred pounds of salt from Frankfurt, for I want her to have something as a remembrance of me."

Mr. Sesemann now beckoned to the children that it was time to be off. Grandmamma's white horse had been brought up for Clara, and the little girl proudly rode off beside her father.

Heidi ran to the far edge of the slope and continued to wave her hand to Clara until horse and rider disappeared.

* * * * * *

And now the bed has arrived, and grandmother is sleeping so soundly all night that she is sure to grow stronger.

Grandmamma, moreover, has not forgotten how cold the winter is on the mountain. She has sent a large package of warm clothing of every description, so that grandmother can wrap herself round and round, and will certainly not shiver with cold now as she sits in her corner.

There is a great deal of building going on at Dörfli. The doctor has arrived, and, for the present, is occupying his old quarters. He has bought the old house that Uncle and Heidi live in during the winter. The doctor is having part of the old house rebuilt for himself, and the other part repaired for Uncle and Heidi. The doctor knows that Uncle is a man of independent spirit, who likes to have a house to himself. Quite at the back a warm and well-walled stall is being put up for the two goats, and there they will pass their winter in comfort.

The doctor and Uncle are becoming better friends every day. As they walk about the new buildings to see how they are getting on, their thoughts continually turn to Heidi, for the chief pleasure to each in connection with the house is that they will have the lighthearted little child with them there.

"Dear friend," said the doctor on one of these occasions as they were standing together, "you will see this matter as I do, I am sure. I share your happiness in the child as if, next to you, I was the one to whom she most closely belonged. I wish also to share all responsibilities concerning her and to do my best for the child. I shall then feel I have my rights in her, and shall look forward to her being with me and car-

ing for me in my old age, which is the one great wish
of my heart. She will have the same claims upon me
as if she were my own child, and I shall provide for
her as such, and so we shall be able to leave her without anxiety when the day comes that you and I
must go."

Uncle did not speak, but he clasped the doctor's
hand in his, and his good friend could read in the old
an's eyes how greatly moved he was and how glad
and grateful he felt.

Heidi and Peter were at this moment sitting with
grandmother. Heidi had so much to tell, and the
others to listen to, that they all three got closer and
closer to one another, hardly able to breathe in their
eagerness not to miss a word.

It was difficult to say which of the three looked the
happiest at being together again, and at the recollec-
tion of all the wonderful things that had happened.

Then at last the grandmother spoke. "Heidi, read
me one of the hymns!" she said. "I feel I can do
nothing for the remainder of my life but thank
the Father in Heaven for all the mercies He has
shown us!"